When Things Go Wrong

Sixteen short stories about innocence

Elaine Whitesides

First published 2019

Amazon KDP

ISBN: 9781791759742

About the author

Elaine Whitesides found herself back in school at the age of thirty, and stayed there for another twenty five years. During this second stint, instead of avoiding games and attempting to smoke in the toilet, she tried to instil a love of English literature into many hundreds of teenagers, and she promoted the use of correct spelling and punctuation, especially the apostrophe. To make a change, Elaine also worked as wellbeing advisor and stress-management consultant at a health hydro in the English Midlands. This exposed her to the problems and pleasures of hundreds of women, giving insights which she weaves into her stories. She has written two novels, a book about stress management for women, a memoir of her childhood, and this collection of short stories. Nowadays she mostly enjoys being a granny.

*

Also by Elaine Whitesides

THE FAMILY OF LOST FATHERS

CONSEQUENCE

THE BAIRN (a memoir)

THE INSTINCTIVE WOMAN
(stress management for women)

Contents

Growing Up

Victor Burrows' coffin workshop was in a place where an old village had been engulfed by the spread of the city. Carole, Joan and I used to walk past it on our way home from school. The street of shabby nineteenth century houses ran parallel with the river, here and there a narrow alley between them showing the cranes of the shipyard, or a glimpse of the oily movement of the water. On warm days, the air carried the rich aroma of the fish sheds, cut through by the lemon sharpness of the gulls' cries. But it was a respectable area, because of the ancient church and the bigger houses around it.

We were supposed to come home on the bus, but about once a week we pooled our bus money to buy a packet of cigarettes, and walked. Then we had to find a place to hide while we smoked them, as our school was a posh one, and the dark green uniform would be recognised. I was there on a scholarship, and I knew that if I got into big trouble, perhaps expelled, my parents would be so hurt. Once, on the bus, a boy from the grammar school grabbed my hat and threw it out of the window. I swore at him, and the next morning Miss Barton, the headmistress, sent for me because she had received a complaint from a member of the public. It's a long time ago. Not like it is nowadays, when if it's just swearing you're quite relieved!

This is how we were when we were near enough fourteen, Joan and I, Carole a year older. She was in our form though, because her father had just left the army and she had been at school in Germany. Her parents wanted to make sure she passed all her O-levels, so she came into our school a year below her age. Joan and I thought she was very sophisticated, being nearly fifteen and having lived on the continent.

Most times when we smoked we went down the alley alongside the coffin workshop. We knew what was made there because sometimes the big sliding door was open a crack, and you could just see in. We walked on then. We told each other it was because we mustn't be seen, but I think it was mainly because we were a bit nervous of the coffins. I was anyway.

At the top of the alley, on the corner where the workshop premises met the street, there was an old shop front. The windows were white-washed over, but we knew that it was used as a store for the coffin wood. Victor Burrows wasn't an undertaker, he just made the coffins. He was well-known for it, especially if, like me, you had a family that included four grandparents and seven great aunts, all living within cup of tea distance, as my mother used to put it. If one of them wasn't well, or in need of sympathy, remarks would be made about soon providing work for Victor Burrows. Given that he was so well known to all the old aunties, I assumed he was old too, so I was a bit surprised when I first met him. It turned out I was right and wrong, because his father had also done the coffin-making before him.

It was November, quite cold. I had just had my fourteenth birthday, and I had a bit of money left, so I treated the girls to a packet of cigs. When we got to the top of the alley, for a moment I thought we had gone wrong, because it was so different. The little shop front was painted shiny black, the whitewash was gone from the windows, and dim lights shone through white café curtains. Above the door swung a new sign, Dead End

Coffee Bar. We were intrigued. Coffee bars were all the rage then, if you remember. Everyone our age wanted to go to London to see the 2i's where Cliff Richard and Tommy Steele were discovered. Pubs were for men and old people. So, we peeped over the top of the café curtains and saw an interior of shiny wood and brass lamps. The space was divided by pine settles into separate booths, four on each side. At the furthest end a counter top displayed an array of white mugs of various sizes, and, most sophisticated of all, a shiny chrome machine for making coffee, steaming slightly. Dimly, we could hear 'Only the Lonely' playing from inside. The place seemed to be empty of people, except for a pair of trousered legs sticking out from one of the booths. Stunned, we ducked down below the windows and crouched, staring at one another open-mouthed, the white mist of our breath mingling between our faces. When the door opened beside us, I think we all intended to jump to our feet and run, but we kind of waited for each other so it didn't happen. We just felt stupid, hunkered there staring up at this bloke, grinning down at us.

'In you come,' he said. 'Gotta start somewhere. It might as well be you.' I wanted to laugh, because he was putting on a bit of an American accent, but the Geordie showed through. Still, up we got and sidled in. It was warm in there, and there was a smell of coffee that wasn't at all like what we had at home, that we called Nescaffy.

'Coffee or hot chocolate?' he asked. 'On the house, as you're the first.'

'We're not kids. We'll have coffee,' said Carole, managing to sound fairly cool. The coffee came in tall white mugs, with a little jug of hot milk on the side, and sugar lumps in packets.

'I'm Vic Burrows,' the bloke said. That's when I was surprised, because I thought that name belonged to an old man. This one wasn't exactly young, but he was good-looking in a filmstar-ish way, with a wave of blond hair at the front and very white teeth.

Carole pointed at us. 'Joan, Eileen, and I'm.. Carola.' Joan gave a little gasp of surprise, and Carole shot her a mean look.

'You're very welcome, girls. It's my grand opening tonight, so you're a bit ahead of the game. Did you see my adverts?'

'Just passing, so we thought we'd look in.' Carole had become our spokesperson. Joan and I hid behind our mugs, trying to feel a bit more grown-up. Vic passed round a pack of Balkan Sobranies, those cigarettes in black paper with gold at the tip. A bit more upmarket than the Embassies we usually smoked. I say usually, but as far as I was concerned it was about two a week.

That's how we got to walking home most afternoons, and stopping off at the Dead End for coffee. I told my mother what we were doing, and said it was so we could talk about our homework now we were in the O-level sets. She didn't really know what that meant, and coffee was safe enough, so we would stay there till about five thirty and I would get home just in time for tea. By this time the place was quite popular, but mostly at weekends and later in the evening. At quarter past four we were often the only ones there.

Carole had a massive crush on Vic; it was Vic this and Vic that all day until it was a bit boring. She carried a lipstick and Rimmel mascara, a little block that you spat on then worked it up with a brush, and dolled herself up on the move, using a mirror broken off an old powder compact. I thought it looked a bit daft with her school uniform. At least I think I did; looking back, I probably thought it was quite glamorous.

Vic lived in the rest of the house above the coffee bar, and drove around in a red sports car, an Austin Healey Sprite. One day, Carole admired it as we were drinking the coffee, and when we were leaving he locked up and said he would give her a spin and drop her off at home.

'Don't mind, do you?' she asked us, only she wasn't asking.

After that, she wasn't as friendly to us. Until then it always felt as if we told each other everything, but now, Joan and I would still chatter on about Cliff Richard, and swap our *Bunty* magazines. Carole walked with us, but had little to say. To be honest, it was a bit uncomfortable because she acted superior, without actually saying anything. We went to the Dead End most days, but now, whenever there was no-one else in, Vic would drive her home. The car only had two seats, of course, so he couldn't have taken anyone else, but Joan and I knew there was something going on.

Joan tackled her about it after a couple of weeks. 'You're not going out with him are you? He's old. Over thirty, my Mam says.'

'Don't forget I'm older than you two. I'll be sixteen in a few months. And I'm not exactly going out with him.'

'What then?'

'Nothing much. Just a bit of fun.'

She wasn't saying any more, so we left it. I partly wished we could stop going to the Dead End, but it was the only thing we did that wasn't school or family, and sometimes other friends went too. It was getting quite fashionable.

Then the next thing that happened, happened to me.

It was a really dark, cold afternoon, early February. Carole was doing her 'I belong with Vic' act and helping to make the coffees, when the door opened and a boy came in that we didn't know. He was obviously a bit older than we were (seventeen it turned out) but not older like Vic. Vic knew him, so I guessed he might be an evening or weekend regular. I thought he was amazingly handsome, not especially tall, but broad-shouldered, with crew-cut brown hair, smooth slightly tanned complexion in spite of it being February. This, we realised from his conversation, was because he was a

14

fisherman, and a keen rugby player, so out in all weathers. He came and sat in our booth, in order to talk to Vic about some 'do' at the rugby club, and I saw his eyes, golden hazel with long curling lashes, better than any girl's. His lips were firm, quite full, and one front tooth crossed slightly over the other. The only imperfect thing was that he had his right arm in a sling.

Vic introduced us. 'Eddy, this is Eileen and Joan.' He didn't mention Carole, and I noticed a few minutes later that he already knew her name. She must have been going in there without us at other times, then.

'Nice to meet you, Eileen and Joan. Can't shake hands because I've got a broken wing.' Instead he put his good arm round my shoulders and gave me a quick squeeze. I was in love. For half an hour he sat with that arm along the back of the seat, not touching me, but I told myself I could feel the warmth of it because it was so close. The injury was a broken collar bone from rugby, and he knew Vic because he was building his own boat and Vic had loaned him some of the coffin making tools. He was talking about wanting to get off the fishing boats, and running his own sailing school.

After that I saw Eddy often enough around the town, and he was easy to find down at the quay, always friendly but nothing more. For a while he had a girlfriend who was in the sixth form at our school, and I used to look at her with envy and hopelessness. She was pretty and raven-haired, clever and athletic.

Meanwhile we saw less and less of Carole, though she was often in the Dead End. Sometimes the red car would be waiting for her after school, and by the time Joan and I had walked there, the two of them were cosying up behind the bar. Vic gave her a Saturday job, and from one or two things she said it was obvious she didn't just stay in the coffee bar when she was with him, she was familiar with his living quarters too.

It seemed ages since we first started going in there, but it was only in March that Carole suddenly said she wasn't going any more. She was bored with it, she said. I thought it might have had something to do with the fact that she spent more time behind the bar making the drinks, while Vic sat with the customers, especially two girls from the secondary modern, Jackie and Doreen, fourteen same as us, but with more make-up and hair-do's. To my surprise, soon after Carol made her pronouncement, Vic asked me if I wanted a job, not her Saturday one, which Jackie took on, but Wednesdays and Fridays, just the time between school and when the evening clientele came in. He said he would pay me a pound, which was twice my regular pocket money, so I jumped at it. I didn't even have to mention it at home, because I was still back soon after six, and he said I needn't change out of my uniform. It just freed him up to chat to clients, he said, if he didn't have to work the coffee machine.

So that's the way it worked for a while. He was kind of nice and friendly, and we got on well. At first I didn't really notice how he touched me, a friendly squeeze, a pat on the bum. That was normal in those days, remember. Then he made a jokey remark about me growing little tits, which I was, a bit later than some my age, but I was always skinny. One day, we were both standing behind the bar, me tidying the pile of mugs, him chatting to a customer, when he started slowly pulling my skirt up, unseen of course. I was scared, didn't know what to do, so did nothing. He got to the leg of my pants, and I could feel his finger just stroking round the

17

edge of my bottom. Then the customer got up to go, and he stepped away.

'Saucy little madam,' he whispered to me. Was it my fault, then?

The next time, I was standing with my back to the counter, waiting for the machine to brew. 'Stay where you are,' he murmured, and this time the finger reached right in and tickled my private parts, only for a moment or two.

There was no-one I could ask about this. Was it the start of being grown up? Joan seemed such a kid, with her *Bunty* and *Girls Crystal*. I thought about Carole, but she was still too mad about being thrown over, and not really my friend any more. The idea of speaking about it to my mother didn't even occur to me. And I'm ashamed now to say it, even to myself, but I didn't want to give up the pound a week. So I just let it happen, until he kept suggesting that we go upstairs, then I knew it would have to stop.

After that, life went on; working hard at school, a bit more social life, a couple of boyfriends from the grammar school, then leaving school. Victor Burrows was almost forgotten, or I didn't want to remember that little knot of guilt and embarrassment in the back of my mind.

The next big change came about ten years later. I was nursing by then, in Casualty at the Royal Infirmary. The doors opened, and in came the paramedics (ambulance drivers in those days) with a man in a wheelchair. It was Eddy! Another rugby injury, torn knee ligaments this time.

'Little Eileen!' he exclaimed, seeming pleased to see me in spite of the pain in his leg. So that's how we met again, only this time he was just as interested in me. We were married in 1972, and had nearly thirty five years together, as happy as any couple deserve to be. The sailing school never really got under way, excuse the pun, because he found he enjoyed building the boats even more than sailing them. He made a very good living at it, and our two sons have happily followed him into the business.

It was in 2002 that those old days came back to haunt me a bit. Eddy was reading the paper, when he gave a little cry of surprise. 'Hey, I knew this chap years ago,' he said. There was a big photograph of an old man, droopy jowls and a flop of grey hair, over a headline 'Paedophile

Lifer Dies in Jail.' It was Victor Burrows all right, just about recognisable.

'Didn't you go into his place sometimes, that coffee bar he had just up from the old quay?' Eddy asked.

'I can't remember,' I said, ashamed of myself.

So I didn't think about it too much. Only now that Eddy's died, I've gone over it again in my head and wondered if I could have done anything different.

Mind Game

This is a story about how one young woman made a decision about her life, her ambition, and how best to be rich and happy. It cannot be taken as an example to be followed by other girls; at least, it would succeed only for those few who share her determination, a certain unusual gift, and a willingness to suspend moral considerations in pursuit of a goal. The success that she enjoyed brought a degree of fame, so to preserve her anonymity, let us call her Patsy.

Patsy regarded the upcoming football season as an educational process. Never having taken any interest in the game previously, she now realised that this concentrated opportunity to learn about it was an unmissable step along the road to achieving her ambition. In July, she bought a book of the rules. During quiet times in the library where she worked, she studied the neat pictures and diagrams, showing the dotted trajectory of the ball from various parts of the pitch, and read with earnest concentration descriptions of tackles fair and foul, strategies of defence and attack, and analyses of referees' decisions. Amongst the DVDs available for borrowing from racks near her desk she found films of important matches from the past, took them home and watched them with the rule book on her lap, often skipping back through the scenes to clarify a point, or, as her expertise and confidence in her knowledge grew, to disagree with the ref. After a while, to her surprise, she found that she was appreciating and even enjoying the skill that was being shown on the pitch. More importantly, she could recognise most of the players, knew the clubs they played for currently, and, in the case of those who had moved around, something of their history. By the time the opening games of the new season had been played, Patsy was confident that she could take her place as an informed member of the footballing world.

Now that her general knowledge of the game was well established, Patsy made her study more specific. Her attention shifted to one particularly famous London club, best kept nameless in this story, in case of being able to identify the characters involved. She felt she may need to claim to have supported this club over several seasons. Fortunately, a yearbook was produced annually, and copies were kept in the library, so Patsy borrowed these and made them her bedtime reading for a week or two. She decided that it was necessary only to be deeply familiar with the previous two seasons, but that she should have a reasonable knowledge of two or three prior to that. This kind of study was not as interesting as the filmed matches had been, but there were impressive action photos in the books, many of which held a strong fascination for her.

Other archive documents proved to be useful. Patsy had access to electronically stored news items, and a few of these were sufficient to give her an insight into certain aspects of the way in which a certain famous footballer was inclined to lead his life off the pitch. Some of this made uncomfortable reading for Patsy, but she could convince herself that it was unimportant in the longer term, and she concentrated instead on the more reassuring topics, such as the untold riches these young men euphemistically referred to as their wages.

The reason for all of this preparation was that Patsy had decided to become a footballer's wife. As a career it promised a good deal more interest and reward than anything more usually attainable by a moderately intelligent, socially gauche, history graduate of average looks. Patsy was aware of her shortcomings, one of which was never having moved in the sort of circles frequented by footballers. Her lack of knowledge of her potential husband's working life had been remedied, and she had a plan that should help her to make the right kind of contacts.

As a result of the attention she was paying to the activities of the players, other subjects for Patsy's attention began to crop up. She was, for a while, disturbed by what she learned about WAGs, the Wives and Girlfriends. On the morning news programme there was a short item showing a group of these women shopping in a northern city, slinking along a street of exclusive shops, their long bare legs glossy and tanned, décolletages tantalisingly revealing, sleek hair swinging shiningly around their perfectly made-up faces. For the purposes of the film they were touting large carrier bags bearing the names of expensive fashion houses. As an experienced shopper, albeit of the chain-store variety, Patsy could see that these bags were probably empty, or contained small items of very lightweight material. In any case, limousines were probably standing by into which the spoils could be dumped immediately. No grooved fingers or aching backs for these ladies!

Patsy hurried home during her lunch break in order to catch and record this snippet of film. Afterwards she compared herself with the projected images. She too was slim, but had little to reveal even in the lowest neckline. She was of average height, and though her legs were individually of a fairly pleasing shape, when placed next to each other there was, she had to admit, a bit of a gap between her knees. Pretending to be wearing the highest possible heels, she tiptoed around her living room, attempting to emulate the slinkiness. Some practice with actual shoes would probably bring about an improvement in this skill, she decided, and turned her attention to other aspects of her appearance. Her hair was blonde, but its paleness rather matched the paleness of her skin, so that the best word to describe her was 'colourless'. Patsy was honest about this, and contemplated the idea of fake tan, or an emergency Mediterranean holiday. The holiday would be a waste of scarce resources, she decided, and tanning lotion was notoriously difficult to apply without danger of acquiring orange stripes. No, she would stick to the crucial strategy at the centre of her plan.

By the time the season had turned towards the Spring, Patsy felt that the technical part of her preparation was complete. She had done better than she had anticipated, hardly needing to study the games in order to expand her knowledge. She had watched, and enjoyed, concentrating when possible on the performances of one particular player.

Now it was time for the next phase of Patsy's plan to swing into action. Rather than go to matches, she studied the routines of match days, finding that when 'her' team played away from home, to protect them from over-enthusiastic fans, they were driven as near as possible to the players' entrance in a black coach with tinted windows. Usually this meant there was a limited opportunity to get as close as Patsy needed to be. For the next away game, she arrived very early, and took her place behind the short metal barrier bordering the walkway between coach park and players' door.

The target of Patsy's affection was the young Norwegian striker; let's call him Lars. Her choice had not been random, but inspired by a newspaper article the previous Spring describing the very good work Lars had been doing at an inner London primary school near his club, dropping in unheralded from time to time to coach underprivileged children. Although the report suggested that Lars maybe needed the good publicity to rehabilitate his reputation after a couple of ugly outbursts on the pitch, Patsy preferred to give him the benefit of the doubt, on the basis that she had fallen immediately in love with his startling blue eyes and strongly muscled legs. After that, she had avidly collected posters and photographs, confirming Lars' extreme good looks.

Lars already had a girlfriend, Jodie, but Patsy was not worried about this. She had read that one of the spats on the pitch was with an opposing player, Jose Mulroy, who had attempted to oust Lars in the girl's affections at a London nightclub. Jodie had been quoted as saying that she was flattered, but that her loyalty was to Lars. This, Patsy felt sure, would not last long. Jodie would soon begin to notice how handsome Mulroy looked, and how he was perhaps in the running for the captaincy of England.

Patsy waited patiently against the barrier that corralled the fans at the players' entrance. When the coach arrived she would be in the perfect position to be seen by Lars as he strode the short distance to the gate. There would be a wait of an hour or more, but Patsy knew it would be worth it to be so close. Craning her neck to see through a crowd would not have been so effective. Then to her surprise, after only half an hour, a large car with dark tinted windows drew up, and out got three young women, much alike with their scanty clothes, swingy hair and golden sandals. One was Jodie, recognisable by the length of her tanned legs, the slenderness of her whole body, and the perfection of her gleaming smile. All three appeared not to notice the waiting crowd that had gathered behind and around Patsy, but nor were they in a hurry to complete the short journey to the gate. Patsy was alert and patient in her pole position, and at the last moment, she caught, and held, Jodie's eye. The contact lasted just a second or two, but there was something in Patsy's look that sent the other girl on her way with an expression of disquiet, even anxiety, on her face.

Patsy was pleased. Now she needed to have the same good fortune with Lars. This was more difficult. When the coach arrived, first a group of tough looking men, minders or perhaps trainers, disembarked, then the players, most of them hurrying through to avoid the outstretched clutching hands of the fans. Lars was near the end of the procession, but she could see that he would be ushered rapidly past. It was not enough that she had the opportunity to be within a few feet of him for the first time, though her heart quickened with excitement as she saw his blond head appear in the doorway of the coach. He must notice her, no matter what. So Patsy leaned hard on the metal barrier, making space and glancing briefly around in the hope of encouraging those behind her to press forwards also. At the last moment she tipped herself over and fell awkwardly into the path of the hurrying players. It was not Lars who picked her up and manhandled her out of the way, but one of the coaching team, stationed in front of the barrier to encourage the rapid passage of the players. But it was enough. Lars had looked down, startled, as she rolled at his feet, and she had looked up into his eyes. He had noticed her, and he would remember. Patsy went home, satisfied.

Lars did remember Patsy. He had been startled as the girl had apparently fallen over the barrier, and instinctively moved to help her to her feet. Before he could reach her, she had been hauled out of his path, but he had been struck by the expression in her pale, round eyes as she stared back at him over her shoulder, her smooth blond hair flicking across her face as she was dragged to her feet. As he walked into the dressing room, he thought how strange it was that although he had looked into her eyes for only a moment, he had such a strong impression of a serene, thoughtful face, not beautiful at all, but natural, the face of a girl who would listen to you, support you, share your interests. Not a girl obsessed with her own appearance, bent on spending as much of your money as she could lay her hands on. He stopped himself, smiling but puzzled. That wasn't the way he thought; he liked beautiful sexy girls, he liked money and luxury, and he liked Jodie. She was welcome to spend.

Lars did not play particularly well that day. He was distracted, not by thoughts of Jodie, or even by that disturbing first encounter with Patsy, whom, in fact, he had forgotten after those few moments of rather aberrant thought. His preoccupation was caused by a telephone message he had received not long before setting off for the match. His sister had called to say that their mother had been taken ill that morning. She had suffered a mild stroke and was in hospital in Oslo. Although Astrid's description of her condition was reassuring enough, Lars had already been granted permission by his manager to fly out the next afternoon for a brief visit. Having missed two opportunities to score during the first half, he was taken off, spoken to firmly but sympathetically and spent the rest of the game watching disconsolately from the sidelines. What he did not know was that one of the team physiotherapists, whose girlfriend was a reporter on a small local paper, had given her the scoop of her life, and the news of tragedy in the Olsen family was already headline news.

'Soccer Star to Fly to Mother's Bedside'. Patsy's eye was caught as she shopped for her weekend meals. She took the evening paper from the stand and read the report.

'Star player Lars Olsen is to fly out tomorrow to visit his dying mother,' she read, shocked, but immediately wondering how this could further her cause. 'Ingeborg Olsen, 53, suffered a devastating stroke last night and is fighting for her life in an Oslo hospital. Her son, star of

Norway's national team, and of … (a well-known London club), will rush to her side, taking the first possible flight tomorrow morning. Olsen, whose good looks and beautiful girlfriend, model Jodie Aston, keep him in the public eye, will be back for his regular training session on Tuesday. Sources at the club say that he exchanged strong words with his manager, who said he could not be spared for long enough to find out whether his mother will live or die. This on top of Olsen's recent shock when it seemed that the gorgeous Jodie had been enticed by rugged mid-fielder Jose Mulroy, a misunderstanding apparently, but one which has resulted in punch-ups between the two players on and off the field.'

Patsy walked home thoughtfully. She assumed that Lars would fly from Gatwick, as he lived just south of Reigate. How many flights to Oslo could there be during a Sunday afternoon? Searching the internet, she found to her surprise that there were no flights between Gatwick and Oslo. Heathrow then. Guessing that Lars would use Scandinavian Airlines, and prefer a direct flight, she found three possibilities. The first left at 1.30, then there was one at 5.30 and one at 7.30. Allowing for check-in time she realised that she would need to wait around the airport from about 11.00 in the morning until 7.00 in the evening. Tedious, but worth it if she could just catch the eye of Lars again, Patsy decided.

In the event she was lucky. Not too many others fans had done the research she had done, so Patsy was able to wait almost alone near to the desk where passengers with only hand baggage could check in. This was a calculated risk, based on an assumption that for such a short visit he would travel rapidly and light. Lars, accompanied by two burly minders and pursued by a small posse of photographers, marched briskly through the Departures area just before 11.30. Patsy waited in his path, and just as one of the minders started gently to move her aside, Lars saw her. He paused.

'Hello,' he said, at the same time wondering why he was bothering to stop and talk to one rather ordinary looking girl, and realising again that he saw something pleasing, something gentle and caring in her calm pale face. 'I saw you yesterday, didn't I? You fell. I'm sorry I didn't stop to see if you were hurt. Are you ok?'

'Yes, thanks. It was nothing. Look, I'm sorry about your mother. I hope she is better when you get there.'

'Thanks. Actually the papers got it wrong. It was a very slight stroke. In fact she will probably be back at home by the time I arrive. No need for me to go really, but, you know, your mother…..'

Patsy nodded sympathetically, all the time looking into Lars' bright pale blue eyes. He was even more beautiful close up, she thought. Lars grinned, and dropped his gaze for a moment.

'You're not on my flight are you?' he asked, surprising himself by a sudden hope that she may be travelling with him.

'Unfortunately not,' Patsy replied, 'I was here for another reason, and when I saw you, I just wanted to say that I hope … you know… your mother gets well.'

'Thank you.' Lars sensed again that feeling that here was a girl who would share and support his interests. 'Look, I'd like to see you some time where you don't fall at my feet or we bump into each other by accident. Would you mind if I asked you…?

Patsy looked at him encouragingly.

'Come to our training session next Wednesday.' He named a sports complex in South London. 'We could have lunch together afterwards.'

'Thanks, I will.' Patsy had achieved more than she could have hoped, and needed to relax and gather her thoughts. 'Great to see you. Must go now.'

Lars was swiftly ushered away, as several bemused photographers snapped vigorously at a stunned looking Patsy. She hurried back to her car, mentally ticking off the things she must do before Wednesday; something fashionable but flattering to wear, hair trimmed, maybe a few highlights put in, practise in the high heels.

Lars, meanwhile, smiled at himself a bit ruefully. Never mind. Give the girl a decent lunch, then forget her. So what if she did make him think that he needed something more than money and glamour, something ….. homely was the word that came to mind, and he wistfully remembered his idyllic childhood. The wood fires, the fields to kick a ball in, the smell of baking when he came home from school. No way, he thought, not with Jodie, and laughed aloud at the thought. Give the pale girl a good lunch and forget her.

Of course, Patsy's strategy meant that Lars did not forget her. The first Wednesday lunch led to another, then a Saturday date. Lars was surprised, and briefly disconcerted, that Jodie did not prove to be a problem in this. Before the first Wednesday lunch he had told Jodie that he was entertaining a fan who had been polite enough to enquire after his mother's health. Momentary guilt, as she had not remembered to do so herself, caused Jodie airily to brush aside anything that Lars may present as an excuse for lunching with another woman, especially when he described Patsy as pale and plain. However, she was sufficiently curious to sit in her car outside the ground until Patsy arrived. Patsy, of course, noticed her, and stared, rather rudely Jodie thought, although she was accustomed to being looked at by men and women alike. As Patsy trotted by, Jodie found herself thinking that maybe Lars would be better suited by such an unglamorous girl. 'He's so fond of his own good looks' she thought, 'he might find someone like her less of a challenge.' And her mind turned to Jose Mulroy, who had sent her a beautiful diamond pendant the previous day. She knew she should send it back, but now she thought how impolite it would be not to speak to Jose about it. 'I'll maybe just have a drink with him. He'd like that.' So Jodie's meeting up with Jose happened to coincide once, then again, with Lars and Patsy lunching at the Ivy, then visiting a secluded Cotswold 'restaurant with rooms'.

Jodie and Jose beat Lars and Patsy to the altar, mainly because Jodie, although ecstatically happy with Jose, of course, was aware that media curiosity about Patsy could surely overshadow her own celebration, and maybe that lucrative deal with Hello magazine. So no expense was spared in fitting up the newly acquired Cheshire mansion to resemble the interior of a Venetian palazzo, complete with an artificial canal carrying a gondola in which the happy couple floated to a huge golden marquee to greet their five hundred or so intimate friends.

Patsy and Lars, on the other hand, were married in a beautiful medieval stave church not far from his parents' country home. The Olsens, handsome, blond and numerous, filled the little church. Many were surprised by Lars' choice of bride, though Patsy looked her best on the day, her face brightened with subtle expert make-up, and her hair shiny with the application of new suggestions of honey colours. An orphan, Patsy had only an elderly aunt and two star-struck cousins from her family. One of the cousins, very like Patsy in one crucial respect, struck up a passionate friendship with Lars' younger brother, Harald. Harald was not the most handsome of the five Olsen boys, but he was the most serious, and about to qualify as an accountant, so the cousin decided he was an excellent proposition for a secure and prosperous future.

So, that is the story of Patsy and her successful quest for fortune and a handsome husband. She told me all about it herself one day not long after we met. I do the cleaning in their lovely home near the New Forest. Lars plays for one of the South coast teams now that he is over thirty. She and I stood on the balcony looking out at the very distant sliver of sea beyond the trees, me with a duster in my hand, and wearing the white overall she insists that I wear while working. Quite a contrast to the bronze silk trouser suit that was Patsy's outfit that morning. She isn't a comfortable person to work for, the kind that runs her finger along the shelf after you've dusted, so I was a bit surprised by how readily she talked to me about her early days with Lars, especially as she knows I intend to be a writer, and I'm always on the lookout for a good story. The cleaning pays the bills until I find a willing publisher. Anyway, I'd just been polishing the frame of a big wedding photo she has on her dressing table, and I asked her how they had met. Genuine curiosity, because they still seem an ill-matched couple even after nearly five years of apparently happy marriage.

She told the story staring thoughtfully out over the trees, and when she finished there was a strange, expectant pause. 'Well', I said, feeling a need to respond, 'you did a good job of getting to meet him, but he needn't have taken any notice of you if he hadn't wanted to.' I giggled a bit nervously. 'You must have been fated to be together.'

Patsy turned to face me. 'Oh no, my dear. I don't believe in fate at all.' She smiled, and I looked into the silvery depths of her grey eyes. She held my gaze for a long moment. For the first time I felt her power, and admired it. 'On the other hand,' she said, 'I have every reason to believe in telepathy.'

The Runner

I caught a glimpse of him as he slipped round the corner a few yards ahead of me. I was standing at the top of a shadowy cobbled street in the Old Town, and the last of the evening sun slanted out from the side street just as he turned, flashing off the lime green vest he was wearing. That was all I saw. But something made me step back into the deep doorway of an old house. Maybe it was the strange quiet of the shuttered town, closed after the day. Behind the timbered fronts, beneath sagging red-tiled roofs, the interiors were mostly modern offices. No-one lived here now to disturb the sleeping ghosts. A few quaint restaurants and bars would open in an hour or so, but for now the old place was deserted, except for the running man, and me. The jettied upper storeys of the ancient buildings leaned inwards on the silence with their weight of years.

He can't have called out. There was a sound like a brisk scuffle, then the pad of footsteps echoing away into the distance. Had the running man collided with someone, or perhaps tumbled, recovered, and continued at a more leisurely pace? I was nervous and huddled back into my hiding place. The heavy silence felt increasingly unnatural, and I jolted backwards with a cry when it was suddenly broken by a harsh prolonged groan.

A strange inertia gripped me for a long minute, then I crept from the shelter of the doorway and made my way cautiously to the corner, pressing in towards the walls and almost tiptoeing on my soft quiet shoes. A moment's hesitation, then I peeped round from the shadows into the brighter street. The low sun was masked by the crown of a broad tree growing further down the hill, but still it took an agonising few seconds for my eyes to adjust to the light, a few seconds in which another horrid gurgling sound almost made me turn and run.

The man was slumped against the wall a few yards away from me. I could see now that he was dressed in stylish, probably expensive, running gear. The lime green vest matched the fluorescent flashes on his trainers, and the piped edging to the navy blue shorts. He was not young, maybe fifty, but trim, muscular, a man who valued and honed his body. I could see his face clearly, handsome and cruel with a strong stubbled chin and thin-lipped down-turned mouth. As I looked at him he suddenly jerked into movement with another of the terrible involuntary groans. He pulled up his knees and scrabbled wildly with his feet for a few seconds, as if trying to push himself backwards further into the wall, or perhaps as a vain effort to stand. Then one foot slipped away and he fell sideways towards me and lay still. The movement pulled a thick smear of blood down the pale plaster of the wall, and I saw that the knife was still protruding from the centre of his back.

My hand went to the phone in my pocket, then stopped. The terrible events of my past are ever close to the forefront of my mind, so I pulled back into the shadows and paused to think. The thoughts are a great deal longer in the telling than the few seconds that it took for those prolonged and horrible months of a few years ago to flash through my brain. What should be the worst memories are elusive, lost in the fog of booze and skunk that almost obliterated my second (and last) year at

Cambridge. That obfuscation is not, as one may assume, welcome; the memories are present in hideous flashes, sickening enough in themselves, but more threatening as I know that bit by bit they could emerge and damage my stability even more. There is the shouting crowd, a roar of noise and ugly grimacing faces, from before or after the stabbing I don't know, except that I feel that I was myself shouting and whooping out of control, wild, subhuman amongst it. Then there is pictured in front of me a pair of hands, quite still, palms upwards, fingers loose. Sometimes I dream of that image, and in the dream I am looking at a skilfully executed painting in an ornate gold frame. The hands look gentle, almost in a position of Buddhist prayer. As I examine it I see that the most striking and admirable aspect of the painting is the depiction of the blood, shading from vermilion to purple where it has pooled in the palms of the hands with a slick and oily gloss. As I say, I tend to see the image as a picture, but I have been led to believe that they are my own hands, lying in my lap as I sat in the middle of the square, the knife carefully placed along my left thigh.

For now, that is all I remember of the night itself. After that things became clearer, beginning with the hours in the cell in the police station. There, the memory is not a visual image; I sat for a long time with my hands pressed into my eye sockets, the universe whirling around me, or myself tumbling through it in darkness, as I felt my eyeballs dashing about uncontrollably against my palms. By the time of the trial everything had become pin-sharp, to the extent that I was myself as brittle and clear as glass, the sounds and movements of the world pinging off me as from lightly struck crystal. The boy who was stabbed did not die, thank God, so the charge was not murder, but grievous bodily harm. I knew I would go to prison, but at first it was a hospital because of my mental state and the physical frailty resulting from the weeks of debilitating anxiety.

Terrifying as that ward was, with its mad-eyed sobbing inhabitants, the silent hours spent staring at the walls of the psychiatrist's office, the unidentifiable night noises, it became clear that it would have been safer to remain crazy. Mistakenly, I thought sanity would restore me to a more normal world, and as most of my psychosis was judged to be drug-induced, it was enough to have a clear gaze and the ability to converse. So I was moved from purgatory to hell. Within days I was torn between longing for the visible terrors of the hospital ward, and thankfulness that half of my period of incarceration had already passed among the criminally insane.

In that women's prison I had one maddeningly unacceptable feature. This was that I was a 'fucking posh cunt'. Ironically, I had cultivated this to facilitate my acceptance at Cambridge, but reverting to my native Brummie simply provoked derisive obscenities and more persistent torture. Most of the time I was thankful to be locked up. So-called 'association' taught me that with fists and plastic bottles it is possible for a woman to be raped by other women. I learned that there are places on the body where pressure causes excruciating pain but no bruise. I learned that there were women in that prison whose sense of humour was most roused by the sight of two of them holding me down while another pressed her stinking bare arse into my face. If witches laugh, they laugh like that. I learned that warders were adept at judging whether the silent assaults were likely to be life-threatening, and turning away if they were not. And even in what was supposed to be a secure prison there are places that are unseen, horrible corners that it is well not to pass, for you will be pulled in for punishment.

In those few seconds that I stood round the corner from the dying man, those images came back. Not that they had ever gone away, but I kept them under control by knowing that never again would I do anything to run the risk of going back into that hell. Never again was I to be found in the vicinity of a victim of a stabbing, never in future would there be any reason to link me with that kind of violence. There had been times when I had doubted that I was guilty of that first one; I did not remember even a moment of it, and I did not recognise the knife. But this time I knew for sure that I wasn't guilty.

The hand hovering over the phone to call assistance for him would place me and my record next to a dying man with a knife in his back. No-one knew I was here today; it had been an impulsive trip born of boredom. I was wearing jeans and a black hooded anorak and my inherent nervousness caused me to keep my head down and to walk close to the wall. It was unlikely that any camera would give a clear image of me. The man was silent. I was not going to look at him again.

As I turned and walked back the way I had come, I knew that for my survival I could do no other. So strange, I thought, that my innocence should cause me to feel so guilty. Now, it was I who was the runner.

Change of Heart 2016

There was relief in Elton Close when the Sold sign appeared outside number 1. Some dispute over inheritance had caused the house to stand empty for many months and its consequent dishevelled appearance was not in keeping with the rest of the houses. Not that there was a great deal of discussion about it.

The inhabitants of Elton Close were cordial with one another, but not particularly sociable. They were all busy people with demanding lives, and Elton Close, with its neat Edwardian villas and long gardens, was not the kind of neighbourhood for gossiping, popping in, or garden barbecues.

One or two tenuous relationships were acknowledged; for example, Caroline Thompson at number 12 was the widow of John, who had been the manager of one of the wine stores owned by Humphrey Murray at number 15. Humphrey and his wife occasionally included Caroline in a dinner party and were solicitous about her single status.

Judith Fairley of number 8 liked Afra Siddiqui of number 3, but kept a polite distance as Afra was her son's maths teacher.

After a while a painter arrived at number 1 to spruce up the doors and window frames. Two gardeners cleared the paths and tidied the lawns. A removal van came, unloaded, and went. There must have been some curiosity about the identity of the newcomers, but no news spread from house to house.

On a Saturday morning, Afra was in the garden debating with herself whether the daffodils were sufficiently over for the untidy leaves to be cut off. Hearing the sound of a car turning into the drive of number 1 next door, she glanced up, wondering whether it would be appropriate to walk to the dividing wall to greet her new neighbours. A stout middle-aged man wearing a boldly checked country coat got out of the car. Afra raised a hand in greeting, but he simply stared blankly and turned away. His wife, emerging from the other side of the car, looked across its roof at Afra with an expression that could only be interpreted as dismay. Harold and Evelyn Casey waited until they had entered by their new front door before voicing their disappointment.

'Well, that's a surprise,' said Harold, frowning slightly.

'Not a nice one either,' replied his wife. 'Of course she could be the cleaner or something.'

'Don't be daft. That sort don't do proper work like that. Anyway she was too well-dressed. I'm afraid she lives there.'

'So we took on this huge mortgage to get out of Highfields, and you think we're still living next to them.'

Harold shrugged and turned away. He was not unaccustomed to life giving him a raw deal, and sometimes included Evelyn in that category.

They had moved to what in their judgment was a respectable area in the hope of having white faces around them, and he was fairly confident that when he got to know the rest of the inhabitants of Elton Close the one neighbour he had seen would prove to be an unwanted minority. It was unfortunate that she was next door, but as he had no intention of having anything to do with her or any other members of her family, the situation would have to be tolerated. In any case, now that the house move was complete, Harold had a job to do as a local co-ordinator of Grassroots Out, and his first task was to ensure the success of a rally in a couple of weeks time. There were three thousand leaflets to distribute, a banner to collect for his campaign bus, and dozens of posters and placards to position around the city.

Harold began with his own house. He retrieved the 'For Sale' sign which had not yet been removed by the estate agent, and replaced it at the gate of number 1, but now displaying the words 'Vote Leave'. Smaller signs were stuck across the front bay window, all displaying Grassroots Out sentiments; Regain Control of our Borders, Speak for England, Immigrants Out. This last one he had printed himself as he couldn't find an exact equivalent among the official supply, but he made sure it was on the side of the window facing his neighbours.

Whether or not any of the inhabitants of Elton Close agreed with Harold's stance, there was general dismay about the unsightly appearance of his house. More conversation took place over garden walls and in driveways than had ever been the habit previously. Judith went to Afra's door specifically to say that she understood the cruel implication of the positioning of the Immigrants Out poster, and deplored it. Afra, accustomed to having, on occasion, to be more tolerant than people around her, shrugged the insult off. 'Ignorance on his part,' she said. 'I'm no more an immigrant than the Queen,' she laughed, and invited Judith in for coffee.

'In any case,' said Judith, 'he'll have to pipe down after the referendum when his side have lost.'

Afra's husband Jamal, whose sport was cricket, allowed himself to be persuaded into a couple of games of golf with Humphrey, for the sake of neighbourly relations. His natural eye for a ball meant he didn't disgrace himself, and Humphrey wasn't a great player himself, so it was simply an opportunity for the two men to agree that they were rather disappointed in their new neighbour, but that in the long run he was unlikely to be much of a nuisance.

On the morning of the 24th of June a rather stunned Jamal was about to get into his car when Harold Casey emerged from his house, almost running, to speak to Jamal for the first time since he had arrived.

'There now, there now,' he puffed, red in the face and grinning. 'You lot will be shaking in your shoes now.'

Usually Jamal would avoid the kind of conversation that he knew was about to begin, but on this occasion, seeing the triumphant grin on his neighbour's sweating face, he felt suddenly annoyed. 'Why would that be, *old boy?*' he replied in his best upper crust English accent.

'You immigrants, taking our jobs, living off the benefits our taxes have paid for, you'll get the push, you'll see. All you Muslims and Poles, you'll be off where you came from.'

'What makes you think I'm an immigrant?' asked Jamal.

'Well, look at you. You're an Indian aren't you? Come here with your smelly food and bad parking. British people have had enough, and said so. '

Jamal looked at him calmly. 'But isn't Casey an Irish name? When did you come over here?'

'Not me, mate. It was my granddad. Been here generations I have.'

'Not as many generations as my family, Mr. Casey,' said Jamal quietly. 'My great-great-great grandfather came here in 1880 having served in the British army in the Afghan Wars. I am considerably less of an immigrant than you are. I cannot make myself any less brown, but you may wish to consider changing your name.' He smiled benignly and slid into his car.

Harold soon overcame his annoyance and went back into the house to watch with satisfaction as the referendum results were analysed on the television. Best to avoid his neighbour even more pointedly from now on he decided. He did not tell Evelyn his wife about the conversation however. She might be upset by its unpleasant logic, given that her grandfather had been a refugee from Latvia and her maiden name was Lusis.

Harold had to keep his head down at work, he found. The car dealer where he was the manager of the service workshop employed several Polish mechanics and two Bulgarian boys who meticulously cleaned the cars before they were collected by their owners. Harold had assumed that his employer had taken on these workers because they were cheap, and was astonished to hear his boss's outrage at the result of the referendum. 'Unbelievable backward step,' he heard him say to a regular customer. 'Seventy years of peace in Europe, the biggest single market in the world, access to fantastic lads doing jobs that lazy British lard-arses can't be bothered to do. And any sensible person knows that division means conflict.'

Harold's views weren't shaken however. He knew that in a few months when the arrangements were all completed, he would be living in a less crowded, whiter, more English country, and he was looking forward to it. In the shorter term he was excited to see that his hero, Nigel Farage, was coming to address a meeting in the city. Harold felt sure that after all the work he had done for Grassroots Out he would be invited to meet the great man.

After the meeting Harold was annoyed to find that other members of the committee had whisked Farage away out of the back of the building without waiting for him. He knew where they were due to have lunch and decided to take the direct route out of the front of the offices and across the market place. In the square a large gathering of anti-Brexiteers was blocking his way with their placards and loudspeakers. You're too late, thought Harold as he jostled between them on the wide steps of the market hall.

Suddenly, a tall man with a megaphone seemed to be shouting in his face, he swerved away, lost his footing and crashed down the steps onto the pavement. Harold was aware of a dreadful cracking sensation in his left leg. He lay very still, not quite feeling pain, but with a ghastly inward certainty that something dreadful had happened to some part of his body. The pain was waiting, just out of sight, to pounce and overcome him the moment he moved.

A circle of faces appeared above him. Someone said, 'Can you get up, mate?' and he shook his head with the smallest feeblest movement. It was enough; the pain flooded through his whole being and the faces receded into a splintering haze of blackness and stars. He was aware of a loud female voice saying, 'Don't move him. His leg is certainly broken,' then another high-pitched exclamation, 'Oh my God, look. His foot's gone backwards', and he slipped into unconsciousness.

Over the next hour or so, Harold gradually came to himself. He was given pain relief, transferred briskly into an ambulance, wheeled through brightly lit corridors, slotted into machines that scanned his leg, and eventually was able to take in the surroundings of a curtained cubicle in the A and E department of the General Hospital. A young woman with a blonde ponytail and a stethoscope was staring at the pictures of his broken bones on a screen beside his trolley.

'Well, Mr. Casey, you've done a pretty good job of damaging this leg,' she said, smiling at him in a way that failed to cheer him up. 'See here and here.' She was pointing to a cluster of fragments in the middle of the screen. 'That's a nice clean fracture of your fibula, but the tibia is broken in four places and the leg twisted as you fell so everything is rather out of place.' Harold felt distinctly unwell and turned away.

'Sorry, Harold,' she went on. 'We can fix it, but I need your consent to an operation. Unfortunately a couple of blood vessels around the break have been damaged, which is compromising the circulation to your foot. It's already feeling rather cool so we need to act pretty quickly if we are going to save the foot.'

Harold groaned. 'Whatever, whatever. Just give me something to sign and get on with it.'

'Okay, that's good. The orthopaedic surgeon is on his way down to have a look at you, then we'll wheel you off to theatre straight away. Oh, and we haven't been able to get in touch with your wife. Do you know if she's out? Could she be with a neighbour or friend that you know of?'

'Shouldn't think so. She'll be shopping or something', Harold grunted.

Just then, the curtain twitched apart and Jamal Siddiqui stepped into the cubicle. For a wild moment Harold thought Evelyn had sent their neighbour instead of coming herself.

'What are you doing here?' he asked peevishly.

'It may come as a surprise to you, Mr. Casey,' said Jamal, smiling, 'but I am about to perform an operation to mend your leg.'

Harold stared at him blankly. 'You're the surgeon?'

'Yes. Unless you prefer me to send for my colleague. There are only the two of us on duty today. That would be Mr. Kowalski.'

'What kind of a name is that, for Pete's sake?'

'He is Polish, and he has only been in this country since he came to do his medical degree at Oxford. About twenty five years I guess.'

Harold groaned again. 'No, you do it. I don't care. I just don't want to be in a wheelchair for the rest of my life.'

'I'm sure we can avoid that.' Jamal turned to a nurse who was standing behind him. 'We can take him up to be prepped immediately.' He turned back at the curtain and smiled at Harold. 'See you in theatre.'

Harold spent only a few weeks rather dependent on his wheelchair. His leg healed well, and he enjoyed his physiotherapy sessions. Above all, once he had shamefacedly apologised to Jamal Siddiqui he came to appreciate his neighbour's teasing sense of humour. They would never become any more friendly than was the custom on Elton Close, but there were regular cordial exchanges over their dividing wall. Jamal kept a low key watch on his patient's progress, and Harold was not slow to congratulate Jamal on a job well done.

One day in late October, Harold was shocked and upset to see a To Let sign appear outside the Siddiquis' house. How could they be leaving just as he had learned to appreciate the value of his 'not really immigrant' neighbours? he thought. That evening he positioned himself to be ready to question Jamal as he came home.

'It's temporary,' Jamal explained. 'Two years, three at most. I'm involved in a research project in America looking at rare bone cancers in children. Should be very interesting and life-saving if it goes the way we hope.'

Harold nodded. 'Yes, I can see that's a good thing to be doing.' As Jamal turned to go, Harold laughed, 'But I wouldn't get long term tenants if I were you. If that Donald Trump gets elected, you'll be out on your ear.'

Jamal grinned over his shoulder. 'Don't be daft,' he said. 'The American people are too intelligent to do that. Trump's even more racist than you are.'

Retribution

It is the sight of her oldest friend smiling benignly on the other side of the circle that makes Frances tolerate the discussion group. Eight earnest women pontificating on what they call philosophical issues, with differing levels of intelligence, is not what Frances calls fun. But her friend Mary had a slight stroke at the frighteningly early age of forty three, and believes that mental stimulus has a curative effect. They attend the group together because Frances offered to drive when Mary couldn't. Mary is now well, but she enjoys the meetings and assumes a similar response in Frances.

This week they are discussing retribution, or as Frances thinks to herself 'come-uppance'. The group leader tries at first to steer the topic along moral lines; if someone's behaviour defines them as a 'bad' person, is that definition in itself retribution? Of course, before long the conversation is dominated by stories of acquaintances who behaved dreadfully, then appeared unaffected by their moral turpitude as well as escaping any kind of consequence. Another line of debate includes tales in which a morally unacceptable act was followed by a severe though apparently unrelated punishment; for example, a local youth, a known football hooligan according to one member of the group, who contracted chicken pox and was much more ill than if he had had the disease as a child.

For a short time the conversation is a bit more interesting as one member suggests introspection and asks whether anyone can discern a link between their own acts and subsequent unpleasant outcomes. Frances doesn't join in, but does think about her own attitude. Does her scornful judgement of this group mean that she will lose her intellectual faculties later in life? She thinks Not!

Frances drops Mary off at home, refusing the offer of a cup of tea. She has a long drive the next day, and must prepare for an important meeting. Her job carries a lot of responsibility and requires her to travel regularly, not always to desirable locations. However, on this occasion she is looking forward to the trip. As it is near her childhood home on the east coast she has chosen to stay overnight in what she remembers as a comfortable, even luxurious, old-fashioned hotel overlooking the beach.

When she arrives she is pleased to see a placard on the reception desk saying 'Welcome to the Promenade Hotel', as there is no person to issue that greeting.

Frances waits quite a long time, occasionally ringing a small bell that warbles feebly within her earshot, but no one else's. This gives ample time to feel sad and disappointed to see how the place has fallen into shabbiness and disrepair since last she visited, admittedly some twenty years before. When bored with waiting, she seeks help in the bar, where she finds what seems to be the only member of staff on duty in the hotel that evening. This is a young lady working as barmaid, who comes out from the bar to work as receptionist, and who is dressed in a manner as to suggest that at any time she may be ready to provide a floor show also. She is nevertheless cheerful, charming and helpful, and checks Frances in.

The room cheers her up a bit. It is quite spacious, the bed linen is spotlessly clean, and there is, as promised, a wonderful sea view. On closer inspection, however, there appears some residual evidence of previous occupants, presumably a bridal couple. First clue, a vase on the dressing table, empty of flowers but still containing dirty water; second clue, little shiny hearts on the window sill and on the carpet; third clue, a white ribbon bow, such as adorns bouquets, tied to the bedside lamp. Also it is clear that they had enjoyed several drinks, judging from the array of dirty glasses left outside the door. All of this reduces Frances' confidence as to the thoroughness of the cleaning that has been done prior to her arrival.

The small town had changed since Frances' schooldays; in fact her school has been replaced by a small development of bland 'executive' houses. The college where she is to attend the meeting is new, and she does not recognise the address. A street map is needed to enable her to find her way, so she goes downstairs to ask if one is available in the hotel. Yes, on the wall beside the reception desk. But the friendly receptionist/barmaid wants to be more helpful. Surely there is one in your room, she suggests. 'Have you got a pad in your drawers?' she asks. At first Frances thinks she is being accused of urinary incontinence, but no, she is referring to a bound collection of information and advertising sheets stored in the dressing table.

By now Frances is ready for a good night's sleep. At first, the bed seems comfortable, but soon it becomes apparent that it has been made with a bottom sheet that is too small for the bed, which means it is impossible to tuck it in. Consequently, a small amount of snuggling in and a couple of turnings over, to get comfortable, have the sheet twirled into a contortion of wrinkles and creases, of a type that dig in uncomfortably and leave an interesting impression on the skin. Never mind, thinks Frances, just lie still.

Then it becomes noticeable that the toilet cistern, which she has activated some ten minutes earlier, is still filling very slowly, but very noisily. It takes forty five minutes to complete this process, by which time Frances is ready to go again. Eventually, the watery gurgles cease. This would be a relief, except that their absence reveals another noise, this time emanating from a distant lift, an intermittently repeated low-pitched rumble reminiscent of dyspepsia in a very large animal. Sometimes the noise takes on a slightly metallic rattle, like a narrow gauge train crossing the points. Strategy! Pretend you are travelling on a narrow gauge railway in the hope that the noise will recede into the background, Frances thinks. It does not work, but she decides it could be worth recommending to guests in the future who are similarly afflicted. Another strategy! Using toilet paper in a manner for which it is not intended, she stuffs it in her ears. While up and (wide) awake, she pull the bottom sheet into some semblance of flatness, again, a fruitless task for reasons mentioned earlier.

So, having got the bed fairly comfortable, and mostly dealt with the noise, Frances settles down once more for sleep. Unfortunately anxiety about the return of the cistern noise has started to induce a need to flush once more. Maybe a pad in my drawers wasn't such a bad idea after all, she muses. By now it is about 1.00 a.m. and strangely light. Although quite far north, it is not Arctic enough for this to be the land of the midnight sun, and she discerns that the source of the light is the interrogation-strength floodlighting which is bathing the whole of the front of the hotel in a vivid orange glow. No, she thinks, 'glow' is too gentle a word, 'glare' is more appropriate. What could be the purpose of this extreme lighting? By this time it could not be attracting potential guests. Is it to make the hotel look attractive to passing motorists, of whom between approximately midnight and approximately 1.30 a.m. Frances guesses with some accuracy there were approximately two? For a while she squeezes her eyelids firmly together and attempts to ignore it. It is like trying to sleep at midday on the sunniest day of the year. Where is the light coming from exactly? She gets up to look out of the window, and there is a large square trillion megawatt lamp trained precisely on her bedroom window. She feels a desire to blurt out all her secrets to the unseen interrogator who is doubtless sitting behind it. It would have been nice to watch the moonlight on the ripples of the sea, but all she can see outside is this glaring beam. All she can see inside is, well, everything.

Back in bed, she passes some time musing on a certain inconsistency here. On the bathroom wall is a little notice asking her to re-use her towels for the sake of the environment whilst outside the window is this massive and unnecessary use of energy.

After a while Frances reaches the conclusion that the white walls of the hotel thus illuminated are acting as a beacon or warning to ships, and her selfish desire for darkness in which to sleep is unkind to mariners. However, she needs to sleep because of the important meeting the next day. Suddenly she remembers that in her luggage she has a pair of black tights, which can be tied around her eyes to exclude the light. This method is not entirely satisfactory, as it results in a large knot somewhere around her head. If on a side or at the back it is uncomfortable to lie on, and if on the front, the feet dangle down over her nose. Possibly the discomfort of this is increased by the fact that these tights have been worn during the preceding day. So a different method is required, which involves putting the knicker part of the tights onto her head with the legs dangling, and pulling the top down over her eyes. This works quite well.

Picture the scene, dear reader. It is 2.00 a.m.; the sleepless guest is lying very still amongst the tangled turmoil of a tiny sheet, ears stuffed with toilet paper and a pair of tights on her head. Her turbulent brain searches

70

for memories of past wrongdoing that would account for this punishment. Somehow, sleep is still elusive. Then, ping! darkness falls. It is 2.20, and the light has gone out! Next morning, after some three hours' sleep, Frances is feeling somewhat jaded. Too tired to care much about how it looks to be eating breakfast with a visible panty line across her cheekbones.

It is at this point that she remembers how arrogantly, just last week, with the selfish motive of wishing to appear a seasoned traveler, she recommended this very hotel to the innocent members of the discussion group.

Sunday School

'I don't think Jesus is going to want you for a sunbeam, Reggie,' remarked Miss Willerby.

Reggie looked up. It was cold in the church hall, so all the children were wearing their coats, but Reggie had his scarf wound across his face so that all Miss Willerby could see was one round brown eye.

'Why not, Miss Willerberry?' he asked.

'Well look at your picture,' she replied. 'I told you to colour it in nicely, and to write one sentence underneath about it.'

'I did that.'

'No you didn't. You have made the donkey green, and you have written something quite wrong. It's Mary and Joseph travelling to Bethlehem.'

Reggie shrugged. 'You said put what's happening, and the donkey has done a big pile of manure like I put.'

'There's only a pile of… well, because you have drawn it. That's quite rude.'

'Mine's more int'resting. And anyway, I put a polite word. I know a more rude word for manure.'

'That's enough.'

Jill on the other side of the table said, 'He means shit, Miss Willerby.'

Reggie's scarf dropped, showing his indignant face. 'I didn't mean that, Miss Willersbury. I meant poo. And anyway it is manure, because when the milkman's horse does it on the road, my dad goes out with a bucket to get it for the roses.'

Miss Willerby sighed. 'Whatever you meant, it wasn't in the picture until you put it there. And my name is not Willersberry. It is Will..er..by. Can you say that?'

'Yes Miss Willersby.'

Jill grinned across at him. Miss Willerby decided to calm down and ignore Reggie for a few minutes and turned her attention to helping Brian, who was using the correct colour for the donkey, but having difficulty in not covering parts of the surrounding hillsides.

Jill whispered, 'That Methodist church up Marsden don't have Sunday School. They have Youth Club. Our Paul goes there and they have records, Elvis an' that.'

'Yes, but you can't go till you're twelve. I'm going when I'm ten. I'll tell them I'm twelve because I'm tall.'

Jill decided to change the subject. 'You got a TV?'

'Not in our house, but my auntie's got one and she's just two doors down. We go there to watch stuff.'

'I thought everybody had a TV by now. My dad says by 1960 the whole world will have them and we'll start dying from rays.' She pulled a scary grimace.

'Anyway,' said Reggie, 'it's just baby stuff on Sunday afternoon. Sooty an' that.'

'I don't watch that,' agreed Jill self-righteously.

'D'you see that nature programme that's on after tea? It was good last week.'

'Sometimes I see it.'

Reggie lowered his voice even more. 'Did you see those horses last week? My Uncle George laughed so much he coughed and nearly choked.'

Jill shook her head. 'No, what was so funny?'

'There was this man talking at the front, but his head didn't cover the whole of the screen, and behind him these two horses... Uncle George said they was doing rumpy pumpy, and the man in front didn't know. My

Mam said go in the kitchen Reggie, but Uncle George said leave him be, the boy's got to learn.'

'What's rumpy… what you said?'

'The one horse had got his sausage out. I never knew a horse had such a big sausage. It could've touched the ground only it wasn't pointing downwards.'

Jill turned back to her colouring. 'You're just being silly now. Horses don't have sausages.'

'This one did. I saw it.'

Jill appealed for adult reassurance. 'Miss Willerby,' she called out. 'Horses don't have sausages, do they?'

Miss Willerby glanced suspiciously at Reggie. 'Of course not, Jill. Horses eat grass and hay.'

'They do,' said Reggie. 'I don't mean a sausage that you eat, I mean the sausage that a boy has and a girl doesn't.' He gestured towards his own lap.

Miss Willerby was speechless. Luckily she was saved from having to think of a suitable reply, as the door opened and the vicar came in. 'Thank God' she thought, meaning it as a genuine prayer.

The vicar was a man of fifty, tall and handsome rather in the mode of Christopher Lee, but without the Dracula fangs. He was a widower, having lost his wife to Asian flu about two years previously. Miss Willerby had hopes of him, and it was this that caused her to persist in the almost intolerable role of Sunday School teacher. It meant that most of every Sunday was taken up by the church. After Morning Service she helped with the Parish Coffee Morning, hurried home for a quick sandwich, then returned for the company of Reggie, Jill, Brian and half a dozen other less noticeable children. The part of the day that she looked forward to was the couple of hours or so before Evensong, during which the vicar did one or two pastoral calls, including coming into her own home for a cup of tea. He never stayed more than a quarter of an hour, but recently Miss Willerby thought she had noticed him eying the sherry decanter that stood on her sideboard.

'Now children, stop your lovely colouring. Here's the vicar come to take our prayers.'

Everyone except Brian immediately dropped their crayons. They knew that after a few minutes the vicar would leave and then Miss Willerby brought the proceedings to a rapid close.

The vicar rubbed his hands together vigorously, thus reminding the children that it was uncomfortably chilly.

'Good afternoon, children. Just a quick visit today. I won't spoil your fun for long. I know you will be looking forward to Miss Willerby reading your Bible story. She reads so beautifully, don't you think.'

There was silence. The Bible story was indeed a regular item, but delivered in a hurried monotone except on those rare occasions when the vicar stayed to hear it. Miss Willerby said, 'Thank you Vicar. It's Molly's turn to say a prayer this week.' Molly looked panic-stricken. This had been the vicar's idea some weeks earlier, that each Sunday one child should contribute a prayer of their own composition. It would make them feel more involved, he believed. 'Don't worry dear, just tell Jesus what you have been thankful for this week.'

Molly gasped, then cried.

'I'll do it,' called Reggie, and before Miss Willerby could stop him he continued rapidly, 'thank you Jesus for my Mam and my Dad and my Gran and my Auntie Doreen and my Uncle George and for the stick of rock that Auntie Doreen brought me from Whitley Bay and for firewood and for grass and trees and the birds in the sky and everything that you made in the world, and for sausages.'

The vicar raised his eyebrows, 'Thank you Reggie. It is good to hear how you appreciate your family. Now let us all say together the prayer that Jesus taught us… Our Father…' .

Back at home, Miss Willerby wept desperately for a few minutes. Then she washed her face, applied a slick of lipstick, blotted it almost away on a sheet of toilet tissue, and dabbed a little Evening in Paris behind her ears. In the living room she moved the sherry decanter onto the coffee table together with two glasses, wondered for a moment if that was too blatant, shrugged, took a good swig from the decanter, and undid the top button of her blouse.

She never knew quite when the vicar would arrive. Apart from herself she knew that he had only two other regular calls on Sunday evening. One was to Mr. Gray on Cemetery Street, who was so elderly that he always made the same joke about being handy for his next destination. His granddaughter came each week to make him a proper Sunday dinner, and to walk him out in his wheelchair for half an hour in the park, weather permitting. At Easter and Christmas she managed to wheel the old man as far as the church, where once he had been churchwarden. Miss Willerby had met her once or twice, appreciated her kindness to the old man, but found her to be lacking in conversation, perhaps not very intelligent.

The other regular stop for the vicar was to the local librarian, Mrs. Goody, who could not go to church in spite of being an ardent believer, as her husband had been slowly dying upstairs for as long as anyone could remember. On weekdays, when Mrs. Goody was at the library, a woman was paid to stay in the house to care for the ailing husband, but on Saturdays and Sundays Mrs. Goody was tied to the house with him. Miss Willerby rather admired her for her erudition, and indeed for her elegance. A handsome woman, tall and slim, she sported a tasteful version of whatever was the fashion of the moment. The husband was understood to have private means, and Mrs. Goody worked in the library, not because she needed the income, but, as she put it, to maintain her sanity and to keep abreast of world affairs.

Another swig from the decanter meant that Miss Willerby was feeling more cheerful and hospitable when the knock came at her back door. The fact that the vicar always approached along the back lane and came in through the yard gave her a little thrill of expectation, a tentative belief that he too felt that there was something clandestine about the visits.

When she opened the door, the vicar stepped in and past her without his usual rather formal greeting. In fact, when Miss Willerby looked at him she could see that he was not, as usual, calm and dignified. He was breathing rather heavily and began pacing around the room in an agitated manner. After a few moments he saw the sherry and glasses and said, 'Is this for us?'

No need to have worried about seeming forward, thought Miss Willerby. 'May I offer you a glass?' she asked.

'Certainly. Shall I pour?' he replied, then without waiting sloshed a generous measure into each glass, picked up his own and sat down abruptly on the settee. Miss Willerby sat next to him, careful not to be too close. He turned and looked at her searchingly.

'You know how I value your friendship, Miss Willerby. You perhaps don't realise how you have been a steadying influence amongst some... well, difficult times in my life.'

Miss Willerby felt her pulse begin to race. 'I hope I have been able to show my um, commitment to you and … your work,' she replied, trying not to gasp.

'I am meaning more personally.' He hesitated. 'May I speak to you openly?'

'Of course. I would value your confidence.'

'This is a situation that began some time ago, shortly after my wife died, in fact, when I began to form an attachment.'

'One that may prove to be mutual?' By now Miss Willerby's heart was doing uncomfortable little jumps, such as she sometimes experienced when extremely agitated, and a wave of heat had spread up her neck to suffuse her face.

The vicar gulped the last of his sherry and refilled his glass. 'Not really that simple, I'm afraid. May I start from the beginning?'

'Of course.'

'There is that very difficult time when grief clouds one's normal judgement. I was truly not myself in those weeks, and it was then that I first met Mrs. Goody. When one has had a marriage of great and lasting passion… I hope you don't mind me speaking of this… the loss is somehow greater. Mrs. Goody is herself in a similar situation, albeit with a living husband. There was a mutual attraction.'

Miss Willerby felt something like a scream rising through her body, which she choked back with difficulty. 'You mean…?'

'Yes, adultery I am afraid. I have since prayed, and I believe myself to have been forgiven.'

'Do you mean by God, or by Mr. Goody.'

The vicar did not hear the irony in her voice. 'Ah, Mr. Goody… sadly one does not consider the wronged party whilst in the throes. He did not know of the affair, which lasted only a few weeks. At least, he did not know until today.'

'Today!' She heard a hint of the scream in the rising tone of her voice.

'Yes, so unfortunate. I have just come from there, having made what I intended to be my final visit.'

'Final? But you said this lasted only a few weeks after your wife passed on. That must be at least two years ago.'

'That is the case. This evening I had gone to say goodbye and to impart some news that was best heard from myself.'

'Are you leaving?'

'I hope not. But I have a terrible tangle to unravel. You see, I accompanied the farewell with a kiss, a kiss of some passion. And for the first time in many months, Mr. Goody had been able to make his way downstairs unaided.'

'He saw you. Poor man.' Miss Willerby found she was standing, looking down at him.

'Yes, but the difficulty is that he took great comfort from what he saw. Poor man indeed. Living for so long with the knowledge that he could die at any time, his reaction was one of relief. He extracted from me a promise that after he is gone I will marry his widow.'

'Surely that is the most satisfactory outcome. No scandal at this time, and a *satisfactory* wife later.'

'If only that were the whole story. As I said I had gone to tell Mrs. Goody a piece of news that I would not have wished her to hear from any source but myself.'

Miss Willerby was by now coldly calm. She became aware of the fact that her previously racing pulse was now slow and steady, the blood had drained from her face. 'News that prevents your grasping with both hands your lucky deliverance from scandal?'

'I needed to tell her of an attachment that I have formed in the months since the end of our affair.'

Oh no, thought Miss Willerby, not me, please God, not me. Half an hour ago I wanted that above all, but not now.

The vicar looked up at her with an expression of anguish. 'You may have noticed that I left the Sunday School rather more hurriedly than usual. I wished to make sure of getting to Mr. Gray's house before Alison left.'

'Alison?'

'His granddaughter, that beautiful, patient, kindly young woman. I admire her more than I can express, and for a short time this afternoon I was the happiest man in the world. She has accepted my proposal of marriage.'

Miss Willerby found herself unable to respond in any way except for a strangled laugh which she covered with a cough.

'What am I to do? I find myself engaged to two women in the space of an hour. You are the only person I know with the practical good sense to advise me.' He turned a face of melodramatic hopefulness towards her. Miss Willerby sighed, shrugged, and replied, 'Yes I can tell you what to do.'

'Anything to solve this terrible conundrum, and free me to seek happiness with Alison.'

'I have three suggestions. Firstly, stop drinking my sherry.' She took the glass from his hand. 'Secondly, get out of my house. And thirdly, hope that one of your fiancées will feel able to take over your bloody, awful, soul-destroying Sunday School.'

After he had gone, Miss Willerby sat alone on the settee, finishing the sherry without bothering with the use of a glass. She felt deeply relaxed, content, knowing that a huge burden had been lifted.

Girlfriend

After his mother had left, Tom made three circuits of the room, feeling the Braille labels she had put on the fronts of drawers, and on the shelves in the wardrobe. Underwear, T-shirts, Sweaters. Printer paper, Pre-recorded disks, Chargers. Everything identified neatly, and he would have to keep it exactly like that. No more shouting down the stairs 'I can't find... Where is my...?' Tom sighed. He had more confidence in his ability to cope than she did, he knew. He also knew that he had allowed his mother to believe he couldn't manage without her because caring for him assuaged her guilt for the accident that had deprived him of his sight as a three-year-old. The idea of living in a sea of disorder, wearing unmatched socks and inside-out sweaters gave him a sense of liberation.

A tap on the door and a voice he recognized announced Steve, the post-graduate student from his department who was to co-ordinate the small team of volunteers who would get Tom to the right place, sometimes read for him, (maybe even check his socks, he thought gleefully).

'All sorted, I see,' said Steve. Tom could hear and feel him moving slowly round the room. 'You can read all these labels, I suppose.'

'Yes, but I hardly need them. I know where everything is and I intend to be as untidy as every other student as soon as I can manage it.'

'So if you're done here I'll take you across to the bar.'

'Yup. That's a route I need to learn.' Tom hesitated a moment. 'Steve, can I ask a favour? Would you speak to me just as you would anyone else? Like… saying shall we go to the bar, or do you fancy a beer, rather than taking me.'

'Point taken. So, do you fancy a beer?'

'Certainly do.'

Alone, Tom would have been disoriented by the noise and movement around him in the Students' Union bar. With an inconspicuous hand on his arm, Steve guided him to a seat at a table where Jez and Phil introduced themselves, one with a pronounced Yorkshire accent which Tom heard and memorised. Jez a Yorkshireman,

88

Phil possibly posh Londoner, posh anyway. They returned to their conversation about Phil's diving holiday in the Maldives, and Tom relaxed, listening to what was going on around him, laughter, clash of glasses and bottles from the bar, snatches of conversation. A soft arm brushed against his and a girl's voice said, 'Hi, I'm Wendy,' just as Steve came back, putting a pint glass against Tom's hand.

Tom turned towards the voice. 'Tom,' he said and held out his hand. There was a pause, then Wendy took it from a slightly different direction than he expected. 'Sorry,' he said. 'I can't see you.'

Wendy was just settling herself rather close to Tom's shoulder when Phil called, 'Wendy! Over here. I've got you a pint.'

'He's *so* possessive,' hissed Wendy into Tom's ear, standing up with the aid of a hand high on his right thigh.

Voices and movement came and went around him. Tom was skilled at homing in on the sounds that interested him. He could map the space, hearing where voices came in through the door, where the clatter of glasses indicated the position of the bar. He asked Steve to

89

describe the table layout, so he knew that he was sitting in a fixed booth, one of six down the wall opposite the door, and that apart from three tables down the centre, the rest of the room was empty of furniture.

'Most people stand,' said Steve. 'The powers that be reckon you spend less time in here if you are forced to stand up. Doesn't seem to work.'

After a while, Tom concentrated on voices. Wendy was sounding loud and peevish nearby, while Steve and Jez were talking football in low voices. From the adjacent booth Tom heard an infectious giggle and a low-pitched gentle voice say something about Paris and the bateaux mouches. The accent was very slightly of the North East, more likely Alnwick than Newcastle, he thought, the tone sweet, almost musical.

He turned to Steve. 'Who's the girl with the lovely voice?' he asked, gesturing in the direction from which he had heard the girl speak.

Steve listened, shook his head uncertainly. 'Don't know who you mean.'

'There, I can hear her now. Tiny bit Geordie.'

'Oh, yeah. That's Daphne Lawler. Never really noticed her voice. It is quite attractive now you mention it. I've only ever noticed her appearance. I guess you should meet her. She's one of your volunteers.'

'Hey Daphne, come and meet Tom,' Steve called.

Daphne came to sit beside Tom, not invasively close like Wendy, and shook his hand briefly. Her hand was firm, the skin unusually smooth, Tom thought.

'Hello,' she said, and he could hear the smile in her voice. 'I'm Daphne Lawler. I've been looking forward to meeting you.'

'Lawler,' said Tom. 'Isn't that a Scottish name?'

'I think it's Irish originally, but I'm not Irish. I come from way up north. Amble, on the coast north of Newcastle.'

'I thought so. I can hear it in your voice. I've got a bit of family up there called Lawler. They live in Berwick.'

'That's not so far. Maybe we're related.'

'Don't think my lot are Irish either. They certainly think they're Scots, from Edinburgh originally.'

'I bet they think Berwick's in Scotland really too.'

Tom smiled. 'Well, when I used to play with my cousins as a kid they had a sort of terrace at the top of the garden that was supposed to be an English castle, and I was the lonely Englishman who had to guard it.. They were always the brave Scottish warriors rampaging up to conquer the castle and steal my toys.'

'Can't have been easy to defend yourself.'

'Well no. I couldn't see what they were doing of course. But I could throw stuff. And as long as I can hear a noise my aim is pretty good.'

'Fun. Or not?'

'Yeah, they were great really. We spent a lot of time on the beach at Spittal. I've always liked to run wherever there is space, and one of them would tie the dog's lead to my wrist and run along beside me.'

'Don't tell me the other end was attached to the dog!'

'Not usually.'

The conversation was interrupted by Steve tapping Tom's shoulder. 'I've got to head back now, Tom. Sorry, but work to do.'

Daphne said, 'If it's okay with you Tom, I'll walk back with you. I think you're on the next corridor to me. Then we can talk about what sort of assistance you need with the work.'

'I'm good with that. Cheers Steve. I'll be grateful for a shout in the morning, though. Show me breakfast.'

The rest of the group wandered off after Steve, only Wendy shuffling along the bench to sit close. 'Sure you don't want me to stay?' she asked, her voice breathily close to his ear.

'I'm fine thanks, Wendy, Daphne will see me back.'

'Phil's waiting for you, Wendy,' said Daphne.

'Oh, keep him to yourself then,' Wendy snapped, and marched off noisily.

'I suppose you get a lot of that,' said Daphne, sounding a bit wistful. Tom knew he was good-looking, and there had been times when he had no compunction in responding to how girls came on to him. His mother had described his appearance to him, rather grimly, as a warning that good looks would influence how people treated him. He knew that he had regular features, dark wavy hair, long eyelashes and his green eyes did not wander in the way that some blind people's eyes did. He was tall, and enjoyed any physical activity that would keep him fit.

He shrugged. 'Looks don't matter to me, as you can imagine, my own or anyone else's.'

'Wendy's gorgeous, and she knows it.'

'So I'm even less interested.'

They had another drink, then walked back to the hall of residence, discussing their course. Both were studying French and Spanish. Daphne was a year ahead, though they were the same age. Tom's disability had held him back a little, though he had the advantage of being a fluent French speaker because of having a French father. In his room he showed her his Braille texts and audio books. She gently felt the texture of the Braille pages.

'Does it work if you want to read Russian, say, or Chinese, where the written characters are different?'

'You can certainly get Russian Braille. I had a go at that because I learned to speak a bit of Russian, and thought I'd try reading. It was very hard, though, and I gave up. Don't know about Chinese.'

'I can show you a couple of really useful sites where you can download many of the audio texts you will be reading this year. Lots of them are free.'

'Thanks. I used to be able to do that at school, but of course by myself it's not so easy.'

Daphne took a disk of Rimbaud's *Illuminations* from the shelf and read out the title.

'I love this. Shall we listen to some of it together and maybe you can explain to me the palm trees of copper roaring melodiously in flames.'

Tom laughed. They lay side by side on his bed, an earphone each so that they could share the rhythms and surreal images of Rimbaud's poetry.

Soon the two became inseparable. Tom's other helpers drifted in and out of his daily routines, helpful, cheerful, guiding him to meals, to lectures, sometimes reading, sometimes checking his typed essays. But Daphne was there beside him at any time that her own studies allowed. Their intimacy increased, and before long she did not return to her own room at night, tucking herself into Tom's narrow bed as they explored each other's bodies. He was enthralled by her beauty, as he perceived it through the touch of his sensitive hands. Daphne's skin was unusually smooth and soft, and during their slow and gentle love-making Tom would tell her that he was seeking the most beautiful place on her body. She had small firm breasts and a slender upper body where he could trace the perfect symmetry of her ribs, straightness of her spine, then the widening swell of her hips. The inside of her upper arms was so soft and smooth that when he touched her there very gently he could hardly feel the surface of her skin. In the delicate crease where upper thigh met her rounded buttock the softness had a gentle flexibility and the texture of finest silk. He stroked her long hair, feeling the weight of it run through his fingers like water. Delicately touching her face to gain an impression of her appearance he felt soft full cheeks under wide cheekbones, the curve of a round jaw and small chin under narrow lips. Her beauty lay also in the scent of her. She used a shampoo that had the brightness of green apples, and her body and breath smelled slightly and naturally of honey. She was strong. Sometimes she would pretend to resist him and they would wrestle until she held him and sat astride and they laughed into their kisses. Tom was surprised by her strength, because Daphne was small, standing below his shoulder. When she walked at his side, he would put an arm round her shoulders which felt as delicate and narrow as a child's. But as she straddled his body he held her hips to pull her onto him, and felt the round womanly width of her. They were happy.

Tom's only problem, an irritation that he shied away from, was continuing unwanted attention from Wendy.

In the bar she would sidle next to him, ignoring Daphne's presence. Sometimes Tom knew that she deliberately sought him out, as she would be there when he left lectures or tutorials, sliding her arm into his and clinging to his side as if guiding him required the closest possible contact. He tried telling her kindly that he needed nothing much more than the awareness of a presence at his side, even holding her away from him and trying to make a kindly joke of her attention. From time to time Phil would find them together, and his antagonism was evident in his voice. Tom was aware that for the time being his blindness protected him from being openly blamed for his contact with Wendy, but that eventually there would be some kind of confrontation.

One day Tom was sitting in his room, concentrating hard on a Braille text when his door opened behind him. Assuming that the lack of a knock meant it was Daphne, he said, 'Hello, sweetheart,' realising a moment later, as arms slid round his neck that the scent was not of apples and honey, but stale smoke breath and strong perfume.

'Stop it, Wendy,' he said. 'I didn't realise it was you.' He stood up abruptly and heard her take a stumbling step backwards.

'You pushed me,' she said, her voice slightly accusing and threatening.

'I'm sorry, didn't mean to be rude, but I wish you wouldn't get so close. I don't want it.'

'You must be the only bloke on campus that doesn't then. Maybe that's why I fancy you so much.'

'I've been told you're very good to look at, Wendy, but you must realise that doesn't mean anything to me. And in any case I've got a girlfriend.'

'You mean that minger, Daphne Lawler. Good job you can't see her.'

'Don't bother to insult her, she's beautiful.'

'Beautiful! Dream on. She's practically deformed, waddling along on those little short legs with her tiny tits and great fat bum, and every inch of her is all freckled like she had paint thrown at her at birth. And her big flat face, she looks like she's been hit by a frying pan.'

'Stop it.'

'You should know how ridiculous you look when you're walking around with that fright toddling beside you. You must have heard the laughs. The same joke over and over. "You'd have to blind to shag that..." then they laugh their heads off.'

Tom sat on the edge of the bed, his head down. 'I don't know what's more cruel,' he said, 'the things you're saying, or the fact that you're saying them.'

At that moment the door opened again and he sensed Daphne come into the room.

'Everything okay?' she asked, surprise in her voice. Wendy grunted and flounced noisily from the room. Daphne came and stood in front of Tom, her hands on his shoulders. Her legs are short, he thought, realising that sitting as he was, his knees were touching her at mid thigh. He slid his hands from her waist and as he felt anew the fat roundness of her hips and bottom a shiver of revulsion ran through him. With a terrible feeling of sadness and disillusionment he knew that whatever happened to them in future he had forever lost his beautiful girlfriend.

The Lesson

'I don't want to go, Mummy', the child said, but he did not cry. By looking at her steadily, behaving like a big boy, he hoped to show how important it was that she should listen to him. 'I don't want to.'

He was not hopeful. His mother did not look down at him. She stood at the gate of the school, staring across at the knot of children rushing and shouting in their game near the open door. She was holding his little brother Davey by the hand, and the two of them were half turned away, silent and unresponsive as if he had not spoken. The child tried to take her other hand from her pocket, tried to hold her so that he would not have to step out alone into the school yard. His mother resisted gently, refusing his grasp, but putting a hand at the back of his neck, ready to push him away.

'I don't want to go. I don't want to go.' There was no other way to say it. He had no powers of persuasion, only the bald statement of that overwhelming feeling.

When her reply came, it was the same as ever. 'You must go, Chris. There is no choice.'

'Why? Why is there no choice?'

His mother's hand on his neck twitched irritably. 'We have this conversation every day. You have to go. All children go to school. There is no choice.'

'But why do they? Who says so?'

'You go to learn. The government says so. Now get in there. I have to go to the shops or you won't get any tea tonight.'

Chris hated and feared this moment every day. It always opened up in his heart that chasm of insecurity, knowing that not even his mother had any power to protect him. He felt angry with her that she could give in so easily to something you could not even see or understand. Who was the guvver man anyway?

'Please.' He spoke quietly, stroking the side of her coat, though even as he spoke he

knew that his legs were preparing to run, that inevitable dash being the only way of staving off the wave of sickness that rose in him every time his mother failed him in this way. She sensed his intention, relaxed and patted his head.

'You go now, there's a good boy. Show a good example to Davey.'

Off he ran, as she watched him, the rapid scuttling run taking him in a wide curve away from the crowd in the yard and into the open door. Even as she watched, two or three of the boys from the group followed Chris into the school, momentarily anticipating the ringing of the nine o'clock bell.

Inside, Chris crept to his peg, shrugged out of his anorak and the woollen hat knitted by his grandmother. The curly-haired boy he hated and feared reached past his shoulder to take the hat and throw it over one of the toilet doors. But his heart was not in it, and he scooted off into the classroom, leaving Chris shaky, but relieved that his day had started so easily. He would wait a few minutes in the cloakroom, now that he knew the curly-haired boy was already in the classroom. The hat he left where it was. He could tell his mother it was lost.

Ryan, the curly-haired boy, sat next to him in the classroom. No-one had told him to do so, but it amused him to tease Chris and the proximity made it easier. Chris sidled into his place just as Miss Barsby started the register. She frowned at him briefly for seeming to be

103

late. Chris liked the look of Miss Barsby, although he was rather nervous of her. Her dark hair was sleek and shiny, and he admired the shape of her smooth sun-tanned arms. To him, she was a grownup of indefinable age, but he knew she was very young, because he had heard his parents say so. They said it in a doubtful voice, as if it were a disadvantage. He himself was very young, but he could tell Miss Barsby had much more power than he did.

In the line walking to assembly, Ryan pushed him, quickly and efficiently, just as he was passing the library trolley. Chris cannoned into it, it scooted away on its castors, crashed into a table and scattered a shower of papers and library tickets. Before Miss Barsby could turn and see Chris on the floor, Ryan was already helping him up solicitously. 'It's all right, Miss,' Ryan called. 'He tripped, but he's all right.'

'You are clumsy, Chris,' said Miss Barsby irritably. 'Quickly pick up those papers before you come in to assembly.'

'I'll help him,' offered Ryan, looking serious and responsible.

'Thank you Ryan. That's very kind of you. You are a good example'

'Cry baby,' hissed Ryan as the two of them grabbed up the papers, although Chris was not crying. The injustice made the tears leap to his eyes however, and Ryan grinned as he saw the effect of his teasing.

Later, in class, they were doing arithmetic, adding up. Miss Barsby showed them two different ways, one with the numbers across the page and one with them going down.

In the book were lots of these sums for the children to do after she had explained the method. Example 1, Example 2 and so on. Chris could do the sums quite easily at first, but soon they became harder. He persevered, and felt proud that he had a whole page of tidy sums. He sneaked a look at Ryan's work, his neat rows of figures. Ryan slapped one hand over his book, and with the other he pushed the point of his pencil deeply into Chris's thigh. Chris wanted to cry out, but Ryan's vicious gaze stopped him.

'Copycat. I'll tell her you were copying.' The pencil jabbed deeper.

'I'm sorry. I just looked. I didn't copy.'

'You did, you liar. I'm going to tell her.'

Miss Barsby looked across at them. Ryan removed the pencil. 'What's going on over there, boys?'

'Miss, he's copying my work. He can't do it and he's copying mine. I told him he should ask you, but he just started copying.'

The teacher approached. Chris raised his tearful face.

'Whatever is the matter, Chris? You know you only have to say when you can't manage the work.'

'I can manage it. And I wasn't copying. Ryan stuck his pencil in me.' Chris pulled up the leg of his shorts to reveal a small pink indentation in his leg. He was surprised. He had expected blood.

'That was naughty, Ryan. I'm surprised at you. You know you shouldn't resort to violence.'

Ryan lowered his head contritely, showing the soft brown curls at the back of his neck. 'Sorry Miss. I just got mad when he started copying. Sorry Chris.' He turned a sweet sorrowful face to Chris, who desperately wanted to believe in it.

'It's okay,' he whispered, that painful lump gathering in his throat again. Miss Barsby ushered Chris from his chair to her desk at the front of the room, bringing his arithmetic book. But before she began to explain the sums, she said quietly, 'Ryan is a good friend to you, Chris. You shouldn't tell tales on him, or copy his work.'

Chris was speechless. A glance across at Ryan showed that although her voice was low the words had carried across the room. The curly-haired boy was grinning triumphantly. Chris turned back to the sums, and half listened as Miss Barsby explained again how to do them. He stared at the page. There was that word 'example'. He had heard it a few times that day. Abstractedly, he interrupted. 'What is that word, Miss Barsby?' He pointed.

'Example? It means something to learn from. You do an example of the sum, and it helps you to learn how to do it.'

'But my Mummy says I should be an example for my brother Davey.'

'That's the same thing really. She means that Davey will look at what you do and learn from it. It's a big responsibility if you have a little brother who is learning from your example.'

Chris went back to his desk. A glimmer of understanding lit in his mind. What she meant was copying. You watched how someone behaved and you could copy them, you could learn to behave that way. So copying was not always bad.

After lunch the children were noisy and excited. It was their afternoon to go swimming. There were twenty five of them, so Miss Barsby, her classroom assistant and several mothers all went to look after them. Then at the pool there were two more swimming teachers. Even so, only half of the class could swim at a time, the other half watching from the balcony seats, so it took all afternoon. As the class lined up with their coats on, ready to go, Chris tried to get in the half that did not include Ryan, but it was hopeless. The other boy stuck to him, grinning. When he went swimming with his Daddy, Chris enjoyed it, but this was different. Not all of the children could swim, so everyone had to have a coloured polystyrene float to do exercises with in the water. Some of the floats were blue and green, and some were pink. The previous time Chris had hung back in the changing rooms in the hope of avoiding Ryan, and when he emerged only one pink float was left. Throughout the lesson, Ryan kept calling him 'Girly, girly.' And he said to the other boys, 'Look, Chris has got a Barbie float.' They found this overwhelmingly comical, and laughed and laughed, oblivious of Chris's feelings.

The pool was a short walk away, along the blackthorn hedge beside the playing field, out of the school gate, two by two walking carefully alongside the busy road for a while, then into the Leisure Centre. Ryan positioned himself next to Chris, and as they walked he persistently leaned into Chris's shoulder, so he crowded him to the pavement edge. Once or twice Chris slipped off the kerb onto the road. 'Chris, stop messing about. That's dangerous,' called Mrs. Gray, the classroom assistant. Luckily they arrived at the pool before Ryan could do it again.

In the changing room Ryan undressed briskly. He was confident and lively, dancing around naked and flicking other boys with his towel. Chris, although only six years old, was modest. He felt skinny and small compared to most of the others, and slipped out of his pants and into his trunks as quickly as possible.

The children filed out of the changing rooms to the poolside. It was the training pool. In the main pool a group of elderly women were doing aquarobics. Chris paused to watch, fascinated as their loose-fleshed arms

109

and wrinkled chests moved through the water. He glanced at Miss Barsby, with her smooth skin and long firm legs, her tight blue swimsuit. How funny!

Chris did not notice the rest of the class had moved on, some up to the balcony and his group to start their lesson. Suddenly, a violent thrust in the middle of his back sent him flailing and splashing into the midst of the old ladies. As he came up for air he saw with no surprise that Ryan was grinning from the poolside. Miss Barsby came rushing, embarrassed, to apologise and haul him from the water.

'Chris, whatever are you doing? Say sorry to the ladies. Did he land on anyone?' she cried out. 'Is anyone hurt?'

The ladies recovered from their disarray, Chris was dragged out to rejoin his class, and little Kylie Best, whose mother was one of the helpers, sidled up to Miss Barsby.

'Miss, it wasn't Chris's fault. I'm not just telling tales. Ryan gave him a great hard push. Chris couldn't help it.'

Not for the first time that day, Chris felt the tears rising to his eyes, and a burning lump filled his throat. He looked gratefully at Kylie, whose mother chipped in,

'He's a bully in my opinion, that Ryan. I've noticed it before.'

Miss Barsby called Ryan over.

'Did you push Chris?' she asked. For a split second Ryan looked as if he may deny it, then he lowered his chin and looked up coyly at Miss Barsby, his round eyes contrite.

'Yes, Miss. I'm sorry.'

'Why would you do that to your friend?'

Ryan paused. A small slow smile spread across his face as he looked up at the teacher. 'He was... just so... tempting.' The smile spread into a grin, then a giggle. To Chris's amazement he saw that Miss Barsby was struggling not to laugh also. She batted Ryan away towards the pool. 'Don't be so silly again,' she smiled. Turning to Chris, she said, 'No harm done then, Chris. You didn't squash any old ladies. Get in the pool.'

When it was Chris's turn to sit out and watch, he thought quite a lot about that idea of following someone else's example. He could see how Davey could learn things from him like sharing toys, or going to bed without arguing. His mother told him often enough about that kind of behaviour. But he could also see that Ryan got a whole lot of fun out of life by behaving as he did. Ryan could somehow do whatever he wanted because he was brave enough to risk a telling off, and clever enough not to be seen. Chris could learn a lot from him he decided, but he would have to make a plan.

On the way back to school, Chris made sure he was walking with Ryan. The curly-haired boy was prepared to be friendly now. Chris had given him good value that day. Chris was relaxed. He had thought about how he had today learned from example, and smiled to himself while he decided whether to push Ryan into the muddy ditch or the really thorny bushes beside the footpath.

Truth Will Out

Want to have soft hands? Wash them with toothpaste. I started doing this one morning just after my husband had packed his bag for an overnight trip. I went to the lavatory, stood at the washbasin to wash my hands and realised he had taken the soap. Of course, there was new soap in the cupboard, right in front of me behind the mirror, but my hands were already wet and if you touch the mirror with wet fingers it leaves an irritating smudge. You do get more easily irritated by some things as you get older. The toothpaste tube was on the side of the basin, so I squeezed a tiny bit and rubbed it all over my hands, rinsed it off and felt the smoothness. The thing is, toothpaste is ever so slightly abrasive so it exfoliates your hands every time you use it. Exfoliates; there's a stupid word if ever. Invented by the so-called Beauty Industry (note the ironic capitals) to describe products that remove the top layer of skin from your face. Not much removed from defoliate which has a very aggressive meaning.

This thing about getting more irritated by ridiculous things that shouldn't matter does increase with age. I remember one day years ago sitting on a train opposite two ladies. I was going to say 'old ladies' but they were probably just in their sixties, younger than I am now. The journey was an hour and they spent the whole time complaining about silly details of life. Baseball caps worn backwards, ubiquity of trainers, music in supermarkets, the glottal stop, 'language' on TV. Not all of it was reserved for the young. They had a good ten minutes on old men who refuse to wear their hearing aids, but I suppose that was a bit more legitimate because they both seemed to be personally affected by that. At first I thought it was quite funny, then after a while I felt really sorry for them because they seemed to have such miserable lives being constantly upset by things they couldn't change.

Nowadays I know better. To sit with a couple of friends of your own age and have a good old moan about the things that are wrong in your own small world is deeply comforting. I thought a bit about why that should be, and came to the conclusion that it gives you a feeling of superiority. You might be old, but you have the greater wisdom and acuity to spot these things. If only you were in a position to pass on this wisdom, the world (well your own little world) would be a more correct place.

Anyway, basically you can't help being like this. Unfortunately if you aren't careful it can get you into trouble, which I found out the hard way a few hours ago. I went to the cinema by myself. It was one of those live screenings of opera, in this case L'Elisir d'Amore, which I was looking forward to but my husband wouldn't go because he said he didn't want to spoil his memory of the Opera North version with the Lambretta. It was showing where we usually go, the Odeon just outside... well, I won't name the town because I don't want to make things worse, but it's in the Midlands. The cinema is on a sort of industrial estate with a couple of obesity restaurants next to it. Inside it's an Odeon like any other Odeon and that's fine.

I was a bit early, as usual. People being late is one of those things that irritate; it shows a lack of organisation in my opinion. So I had to wait in the sort of wide corridor that runs between the screens. Other (mostly old) folk began to arrive. It's a shame proper music doesn't appeal to the young, but I suppose that's because it requires a degree of concentration and, yes, patience sometimes, and they don't have that. Into the corridor came a couple, about fifty-five, the woman dressed quite smartly as for a middle-class evening out, all made up and with a hair-do, the man in slacks and an Argyle golf sweater. But, and I could hardly believe this, each of them was carrying a plastic tray with those pointy crisps and a cupful of some sort of dip. And they were dipping and crunching as they approached. I had to turn my back. Popcorn is bad enough as it smells, but it's generally a habit of the young and you don't get it much in the sort of films I like. But this...

So, in we went. I found my seat, on the aisle in the superior section, and settled down with the synopsis provided, though I don't need it as the story is familiar to me. Then, would you believe it, the crisp eaters came pushing past my knees to sit right beside me. By this time they hadn't made much of an impact on the crisps and dips which were clearly going to last for at least the first Act. I was exasperated.

'Oh dear,' I said to the woman, 'I had hoped you wouldn't be sitting next to me.'

'Why's that?' she replied.

'Well, I would have thought you could have had your supper before you came,' I pointed out.

'Sorry,' she said, not meaning it.

The man leaned across. 'What's the problem?'

'This,' I pointed at the food. 'It's rather inconsiderate, don't you think?'

'Well I like a snack when I'm at the pictures,' the woman said.

'Are you sure you've come into the correct screening?' I asked. 'This is the opera.'

Just then the lights dimmed, the conductor appeared on the screen and the orchestra burst into the lively opening bars of the overture.

'What's up with her?' I heard the man ask.

'Just a sad old snob. Take no notice,' replied the woman, ostentatiously taking a dripping gobbet of garlic-scented dip into her mouth.

'The opera *has started*,' I informed them. I've noticed before that a lot of people who aren't accustomed to the opera don't realise that the overture isn't like the opening credits of an ordinary film. Unfortunately I said this rather loudly just as the music changed into the quieter more lyrical section that follows the opening. A number of heads turned.

'Oh just zip it, you old busybody,' the man said, even more loudly.

'Yes. You should have better behaviour at your age.' She was nearly shouting at this point. 'Go find us somewhere else to sit,' she said to the man.

He got up and pushed rudely past. By now quite a few people were muttering, but quietly. Opera audiences generally behave with decorum. I knew he wouldn't have much luck, because they always put these screenings on in the smallest cinema not noticing that they are actually rather well supported. Sure enough he was back in a few moments, accompanied by a cinema employee.

'Could you come this way, madame', the boy said to me. 'I can find you a seat elsewhere. I'm afraid there aren't two together for this lady and gentleman.'

I got up with some relief, which was short-lived as he led me right to the front of the standard seats where a few were empty on the front row.

'I'm not sitting here. This is not what I paid for.'

'It's all there is, I'm afraid. This film is very popular'.

'In which case it should have been shown in a larger space.'

By now, and I must say I had some sympathy with this, quite a few of the audience were expressing displeasure with the disruption, but as I was not at fault I was unwilling to give in.

'I paid for a superior seat on the aisle and that is what I want. I will not settle for anything else.'

'In that case, you need to come with me,' he said and started off up the aisle back towards the superior section. I followed, but was surprised to find that he led me out into the corridor. By this time he was holding my elbow quite firmly, I thought to guide me in the darkness, but he did not let go so I had to give him a fairly firm shake to break free. It was not my intention to cause him any discomfort but he said, 'Ow' and flexed his fingers vigorously.

The next thing I knew was that two of them had me by the arms and I was being marched towards the door. As it opened (automatically so they did not need to let me go) a group of swaggering youths was entering, beer cans in hand.

119

'Oh dear, chucking Grandma out, are you,' remarked one, as the two employees rather roughly pushed me through the door.

'Oh hello Hugo', I said, trying to make light of the situation.

'Wha'd'ya mean Hugo,' he replied, not unexpectedly. 'What kind of a name is that?'

'Well if I'm your Grandma, you must be my grandson Hugo. Sorry I didn't recognise you right away.'

'Take no notice of her. She's mental,' contributed one of the cinema employees.

This annoyed me as there are some modern rules of behaviour with which I agree. 'Don't take that attitude,' I told him. 'Mental is not a term that should be used pejoratively. And in any case I am far from mentally ill.'

This apparently caused the cinema employee to lose patience. 'Just get out of here,' he shouted, getting hold of me again, much more aggressively this time, whereupon 'Hugo' took issue with him, and before I knew what was happening a full scale fracas had ensued.

My own involvement was purely a result of trying to reason with them, and attempting to pull them apart as I did so. The policeman has told me to sit in the cell until

120

my husband arrives, and think about how my own behaviour may have contributed to the situation. I did try to explain that theory about the atrophy of certain parts of the frontal lobe in older people which can make them involuntarily outspoken, but he wasn't interested. It doesn't mean one isn't telling the truth, though.

Learning to Dive

Julie's husband Marcus did not understand why she should wish to learn how to dive. Indeed he made little attempt to understand, although, when she told him of her intention, he did ask the question 'Why?'

At the time he was watching Arsenal on the television, and Julie half-heartedly addressed the back of his head in her effort to explain.

'I always said I would want a new project when Helen went off to university. There aren't many places you can learn, you know. They give lessons at Waterpark Pool because there are diving boards, which you don't see in many places.' She looked between Marcus's head and the television. 'And it's sport.'

For a moment he looked round. Being interested in sport was one of the ways Marcus defined himself. 'Is it?'

'Well it's in the Olympics.'

'Can't see you in the Olympics, love.'

Julie picked up the bag containing her swimsuit and towel. She was also taking shampoo, conditioner, styling brush and body lotion. The newly refurbished changing rooms were quite luxurious and she intended to make the most of this.

The diving lesson took place between three thirty and four on Saturday afternoon. There were only three pupils; Christopher, aged nine, Emily, aged seven, and Julie, forty-one. This was a little disconcerting because both Christopher and Emily were pupils in the school where Julie taught Year 6. Neither of them seemed to think it was at all strange that they should be sharing this experience, however.

'Hello, Miss,' they greeted her. Christopher sat on the side of the pool, splashing with his feet, and Emily held Julie's hand while they waited for their instructor, Brad. Julie knew him as Brian Bradley, who had been in her class some twelve years previously, but he gave no sign of recognising her so she simply said, 'Hi Brad', when he introduced himself, and settled into enjoying the lesson.

Their target by the end of this first half hour was to be able to stand on the side of the pool, bending from the waist, arms extended, thumbs linked, head between upper arms, and then tip gently forwards into the water. Christopher was brave and cocky, and jumped in every time with a splash, legs flailing, in spite of Brad's increasingly irritable instruction to keep his feet in contact with the side until his head was in the water. Little Emily instinctively lifted her head and landed flat on the surface on her stomach. The second time she did this, she cried, and her mother came to take her away. Only Julie slid smoothly, breaking the lilting surface with barely a ripple each time, until Brad concentrated only on her, leaving Chris to his splashy enjoyment. Brad touched Julie's kneecap. 'Concentrate on keeping your legs straight now. You've got the upper body position right. You could even think about pointing your toes as you go into the water.'

Julie slipped through the water time and again, aware of the sleekness of her body, the arch of her back as she turned towards the surface. After half an hour Brad wandered off to take his turn sitting on the high stool from which the pool was surveyed for safety, but Julie continued to practice until the effort of climbing the short ladder out of the water was causing her legs to tremble. She was exhausted, but satisfied. The first lesson was a success, and she booked the second, not for the following Saturday, which now seemed too far distant, but for Wednesday evening. There was no time for relaxing in the sauna, or styling her hair. A quick slather of the lotion, a drag of the hairbrush – her elation at the success of her lesson, the smooth obedience of her body to Brad's instructions sent her home tired but buzzing with satisfaction.

Marcus was peering moodily into the fridge when she arrived, although the crusty edges of a pizza and two empty beer cans on the kitchen table indicated that he had kept his appetite occupied during the match.

'They lost', he said gloomily. 'What d'you want for tea? I'll cook it if you like.'

'Has to be steak and chips then,' said Julie, good-naturedly, 'since that is the alpha and omega of your culinary repertoire.' She pointed to the two steaks on a plate just in front of his peering face.

Marcus grumpily, and in detail, recounted the mistakes made by the Arsenal players. Julie was accustomed to this. She put cutlery on the table, sliced a few strawberries to go with ice cream, opened a bottle of Chilean red wine, as Marcus flipped the steaks. Usually she would be mildly irritated by his assumption of her interest in his analysis of the match, and his total lack of interest in what she had been doing. Today, she felt sorry for him, affectionate in the way she sometimes felt for children at school, who got things wrong or suffered little failures through ignorance or naivety. Marcus, who was an accountant, wore a suit five days a week. On Saturday afternoons, tacitly understood to be his time for relaxation, he spent watching whatever football was on the TV, and for this he always wore his Arsenal strip. Julie noticed that he still had good muscular legs in spite of the spreading bulk of the rest of his body.

The diving lessons were booked for Wednesdays and Saturdays during the following six weeks. Brad was pleased by her aptitude, her willingness to practise after the lesson was over, and often commented favourably on her progress. Nine-year-old Chris appeared once more, spent half an hour flinging himself into the water, spluttering, climbing out and flinging himself in again. After that, Julie had Brad to herself. During the third lesson, after she had sprung lithely from the side, hands and heels together, legs straight, toes pointed, and touched exactly the spot that Brad indicated, two metres from the side on the floor of the pool, he had smiled wryly and made a remark about her being a better pupil than he had ever been, showing that he did remember their previous acquaintance after all.

At the end of the fifth lesson, Julie suffered a setback. She was happy and confident performing her neat splashless dives from the side of the pool and from the first and second steps of the diving board, but when Brad asked her to climb to the third step she was suddenly overcome by fear. The echoing Babel sounds of the swimmers pulsed back and forth in her head, the moving reflections on the surface of the water seemed to recede into a shimmering distance, and her head swam in echoing waves. Julie turned and grasped the rail behind her, gasping and shaking. Below, Brad called, 'What's up?'

'I can't do it. It's too high.' Fortunately, Brad did not argue. Instead he climbed to the step below her, took her hand and helped her down to the first step.

'Go from here. You know you can do this.'

For a moment Julie was afraid that the waves of dizziness would engulf her again, but the familiar sight of the blue water just below her steadied her nerves and she flipped, with rather less grace than usual, to skim over the wavering black lines beneath her. Brad told her to dress and meet him in the gym that overlooked one side of the pool. Julie had watched people endlessly running towards her behind the window, but had never been into the room. She saw that Brad had pulled a small trampoline into a corner. After demonstrating a couple of times, he told her to practice jumping onto it, springing up high with straight legs, pointed toes and her arms stretched above her head.

'A hundred times on and off,' he said, and left her without further explanation. Obedient, and intrigued, Julie attempted to comply with the instruction. After thirty jumps her legs were shaking, and she knew she would not achieve more than fifty. Was Brad aiming to improve her stamina, or to overcome her fear of heights? Next lesson, Julie found out. Instead of pushing her to climb the high steps, he took her to the springboard. A step, a spring, and the sleek glide through the water. Even more exhilarating.

Somehow, the diving lessons had made a change in Julie's life. Not dramatically, not in a way that anyone noticed; except perhaps for Amy her friend at school, whose classroom was next door. At first, slightly embarrassed by what she thought of as her own eccentricity, Julie had not mentioned the lessons. Then on the fourth Wednesday, when once again Julie packed up her books, gulped half a cup of tea in the staffroom, and got ready to rush off, Amy stopped her.

'Hang on. Why the hurry? You did this last week too. And the week before if I'm not mistaken.' Amy looked at her archly. 'Is something going on that I don't know about?'

'Hm…yes. I've got an assignation with a twenty-two year old former pupil,' Julie replied, teasingly turning her back to pick up her bag.

'Just a minute. What are you up to?'

'Rushing home to get Marcus's tea ready, so I can go out with a clear conscience.'

'Really? A totally clear conscience?' Amy was still teasing.

'Yes. Actually I have a …swimming lesson on Wednesday evenings, and I don't like to be late.'

'Okay. Excitement over. Off you go.'

As Julie reached the door, Amy called after her. 'Who's the former pupil?'

'Before your time. Brian Bradley. He works at the pool. Instructor, gym trainer, lifeguard and so on.'

As she drove home, Julie wondered why she had said 'swimming' to Amy. But the answer was clear to her, although not easy to put into words. She did not want to arouse Amy's interest. The diving meant something she was not ready to define. It was making her into a woman who was not as ordinary as she seemed; not glamorous, not adventurous, but not just Marcus Johnson's wife, not just the dull reliable teacher, Mrs. Johnson of Class 6B. That was enough, just to know that if she wanted to, she could change herself, a little bit.

On the tenth Saturday, the weather was bad; brisk icy flurries of snow hissed out of a steely sky. Julie's car chuntered and chuntered, but wouldn't start. She had left a door slightly open and the light had drained the battery, but there was no need to tell Marcus this. Reluctantly, he put a tracksuit on over his Arsenal strip and drove her to the pool. Rushed now, she got out of the car, but turned back to say, 'I'll get the bus home. There's one at four thirty and you'll still be watching the match.' She ducked her head down into the car to see him nod his assent.

Julie and Brad worked on her swallow dive. A short brisk run on the springboard, raising the right knee so neatly with a pointed toe on the high spring, head up, body straight, turning towards the water, back arched, face forwards, legs together. The two expanding seconds, airborne, during which the arms were outstretched, then the rush downwards into the few moments of silence. When Julie's head broke the surface, it was to a volley of applause. Half a dozen swimmers had stopped to watch her, drawn by the simple grace of the dive. It was perfection, Julie thought. I can't ever do better than this, my one perfect dive.

At home, the house was quiet. Julie was surprised. Although she was a few minutes later than usual, the commentary, the match analysis, should still be rumbling on, Marcus should still be sitting comfortably in his leather armchair, not quite ready to cook the steak. Instead, he was standing with his back to her, looking out at the monochrome garden, streaks of snow emphasising the darkness of the bare soil.

'You're not dressed for football,' she said, looking at his cords and moleskin jacket, his off-duty accountant's clothes. This deviation from normality unnerved her.

'Most of the matches were cancelled,' he replied, quietly. 'The snow is much worse in other places.' Still he didn't turn to look at her, and Julie heard something in his voice that sent her to his side. His eyes looked red and rubbed.

'What's wrong? Is it Helen?' A terrible dread clutched at her, and Marcus turned quickly to put an arm round her shoulders.

'No, no. Nothing. Nothing to worry about. Sorry. I didn't mean to scare you.'

'What then?'

Marcus was silent, his face thoughtful. 'It's nothing,' he said again. 'The football was off so I came to collect you. Much too early, but I thought I'd just wait around, watch for a while.'

'I didn't see you. Had I gone already?' She wondered why she had come home on the bus if Marcus had been at the pool with the car.

'No. You were there. I went onto that balcony where spectators can sit. It's quite noisy there, isn't it? Echoes. And the pool was full. So it took me a moment or two to get my bearings. Then I saw that the diving pool is separate, and just as I looked, a lovely tall woman walked onto the board, took a couple of steps, and did the most perfect dive. It must have taken two or three seconds at most, but I felt as if I'd watched her for ever. It was as if the time stretched out so that I could see every little movement, the tension of her arms, the curve of her feet, the arch of her body. Then she slipped into the water and disappeared.'

'It was me.' Julie looked up into his face. 'Why didn't you wait for me? The lesson was finished then.'

'I don't know. I was shocked. I didn't know what I would say to you.'

'Shocked? Why?'

'I didn't know you, Julie. I didn't know you could do anything like that, so perfect, so beautiful. How could I have been so uninterested, so uninvolved while you changed into a person who could do something so... moving? That's what it was. It was so perfectly beautiful, and I saw it only by chance.'

'I don't understand. Why is that so upsetting?'

'Like I said ... at that moment I didn't know you. I thought everything about you was completely familiar to me, but every Saturday afternoon you had gone away to become a different person. It scared me.' Marcus looked down. 'Sounds stupid, but I felt as if some part of you had left me.'

Julie turned to stand in front of him, between him and the garden. Things have changed, she thought. A shift in power between us, and it feels good. She put her arms round Marcus, and her cheek against his. 'Don't worry,' she said. 'The diving lessons are over. I've done that now.'

The Anniversary

Unusually, he notices himself in the mirror while shaving. Fifty years unwavering routine and a mind elsewhere than on his own appearance have made him effectively invisible. But this morning he sees himself. 'I am an old man now. Maybe this time I will die,' he thinks, and then forgets.

For as long as he cares to remember his mind has had a single preoccupation, and this morning's distraction is momentary. As always, his thoughts are travelling in an endless, infinitely complex labyrinth of calculation. His life is mathematics, his passion, identity and escape is forever there, turning, seducing, comforting, inside his head.

Fifty years ago he arrived at this university as a nervous immature eighteen-year-old, a mathematical prodigy apparently. All of his childhood was spent on a Derbyshire hill farm, and when his ability outstripped the resources of his small old-fashioned grammar school, he stayed at home teaching himself. The maths department and hall of residence were frightening at first, then became familiar places within which he could invent a new isolation. After his doctorate, when his research was clearly valuable to the department, he was offered a teaching post, and a room in the Hall warden's house. There he remains. Successive wardens declare him to be no trouble, indeed hardly seen for weeks at a time. All his meals are taken in Hall, so he rarely strays beyond the campus. There are words that he hears, referring to him; brilliant, distinguished, inspirational. He is aware also of other words; obsessive, autistic, but he does not care or bother to identify with any of those descriptions. His life is under control, emotion drowned in intellect, the terror almost always kept at bay.

But today is the anniversary, so 'I am an old man now,' he thinks. 'Perhaps this time I will die.'

This day each year is the only one unlike the rest, and today is the fiftieth time. It is a day in which he cannot help but remember the start of the terror. At first, when he was new and afraid, some of the older boys (and they were boys in 1965; no-one was an adult before the age of twenty-one) tried to entice him from his room, taking him despite his feeble protests to the bar and sitting him behind a pint of beer. They were laughing at him, he knew, but had no means of resistance. An older man sat with them. The others seemed to know him, but he was not introduced or explained. A girl came and leaned on this man's shoulder, speaking quietly into his ear, but looking beyond him at each boy in turn. He saw that her eyes were huge, and yellow, like a lion's. He wanted to look at them but was afraid, and turned away, feeling his heart jump awkwardly in his chest.

There was a grin and a gesture towards him amongst the others, and the man turned to him. 'This is for her,' he said nodding towards the yellow-eyed girl, now standing near the door. A small envelope was handed over, passing palm to palm unseen. Seeing an opportunity to escape, he crept towards the door, where the girl stood in front of him, smiling.

'The wild boy,' she said, moving close.

'I'm not wild.'

'Yes you are. You are wild like a rabbit is wild, like a fox is wild. I can tame you. I can make you come to me, like a little animal to feed from my hand.' She stepped right up to him, so that he could smell the alcohol sweetness

139

of her breath, and her lips brushed his. She took his hand for a moment and the envelope was gone. Blackness rushed up behind his eyes and he staggered, almost fell.

For a while, perhaps an hour or more, he wandered aimlessly around the roads of the campus, thinking he would find his way back to his room. Probably this was when the habit of mental calculation began; he could stave off panic by immersing his mind in figures, symbols, strange numerical connections. At last, as he approached the college building for the second or third time, he became aware of two girls at the centre of the inner courtyard, crouched beside a figure on the ground. He recognised that the figure was convulsing. His father's old sheepdog had done that before it died. Then he saw it was the yellow-eyed girl, and bent to look at her. Her eyes were no longer yellow; the pupils were so huge that they looked entirely black. Even as he watched, they rolled and were still, and he knew she was dead. In the air around him he heard her voice as she had said, 'I can make you come to me.'

Now, today, as in all the intervening years, the date of that death is a time of waiting for night. In darkness he begins his walk, up the hill from the Hall, past the great library, to the door of the students' bar, then up to the archway leading into that courtyard. Here he pauses, knowing that the next step will take him from his world into hers. It is icy cold, everything is still, the noise of the traffic on the road below silenced. A silvery shimmer surrounds his vision, everything around him recedes and turns to glass. So he walks on, to that spot where she died. The dark figure rises before him, a shadow as opaque but insubstantial as smoke, and the air whispers, 'I can make you come to me.' There is the second in which her presence against him and around him briefly robs him of consciousness, then he walks on, out of the opposite archway and into reality. His mind refills with calculating the forces that keep the stars apart.

Spoiled

Everyone in the family, including herself, knew that Daisy was spoiled. The trouble was that they didn't think about the meaning of the word. To Daisy it was a good thing to be; she had only to express a passing desire for something, a toy, a chocolate bar, a trip to the latest Disney film, and the treat would appear. Her parents and her brothers used the word alongside an indulgent smile. Our own fault, they thought, smiling wryly, but it can't be helped, she is so cute.

Daisy was the youngest of four children. Her brothers were all in their teens when she was born; 'a welcome surprise', said the parents. Dominic the eldest left for university before her first birthday. He would more or less forget her while he was away from home, then when he returned he was disarmed again every time by her smiles and hugs, her round blue eyes and curls. Daniel, fourteen at the time, took a while to get over his surprise and disquiet at the thought of what had led up to the unexpected pregnancy, then as she grew into a laughing toddler found her a regular source of amusement.

It was David, the thirteen-year-old, who felt the most impact from the arrival of his little sister. He was used to being the youngest in the family, and expected to feel angry and neglected when his place was supplanted. The day after Daisy's birth when she was brought home from the hospital, he was told to sit on the settee so that the baby could be put into his arms safely. Her soft pliable weight settled into his lap and he looked down at her small face. Her dark eyelashes lay on her cheeks, for a moment her sweet curved mouth pouted, then she opened her eyes and looked up at him. The dark unfocussed baby gaze seemed to look into rather than at him. 'She knows me,' he said.

A wave of overwhelming love filled him and he looked up at his mother with an expression of stunned bafflement. She laughed, seeing his consternation. 'Hello, big brother,' she said in a squeaky baby voice.

So, from then on Daisy was indulged almost every moment of her life. When her father was out at work and Daniel and David were at school she had her mother to herself. When the boys came home her allegiance immediately changed and she would demand a playmate, to build towers of bricks to be demolished at a swipe, to run after her and tickle and laugh, to throw a ball in the garden, or to push her buggy to the corner shop for an ice cream or 'forbidden' sweets.

There was a difficult year for her when both brothers were preparing for exams and she was forced to leave them alone to do their homework and revision. Nevertheless she kept herself at the centre of their attention by sitting silently outside David's bedroom door, and fixing him with a pathetic round-eyed stare whenever he emerged.

As a teenager Daisy, though still disarmingly pretty, became less appealing. She developed an unattractive obstinacy and sullenness if her demands were not met. The middle-aged parents, having outgrown the energy of youth, either gave in reluctantly or responded with bouts of frustrated rage. Dominic, now in his mid-thirties, was programming computers in the United States, Daniel as a student had travelled as far as Goa and stayed there. Only David still succumbed to Daisy's round eyes and dimpled smiles, though his exposure was reduced because he lived most of the time with a girlfriend near the school where they both worked.

So it was that one night David and Daisy got themselves into trouble. The parents, attending the funeral of an elderly aunt several hundred miles away, took it for granted that David would spend the night in the family home so that Daisy, now fourteen, would not be alone. Daisy was excited by the fact that David had bought himself a car, an unglamorous but reliable German car, and on a couple of previous visits he had allowed her to drive it on the quiet lane leading up to the house. As soon as he arrived Daisy ran out.

'Let me drive, let me drive, please,' she begged, dimpling sweetly.

'Not this time,' he replied. 'I'm tired, it's nearly dark, and I doubt whether you are going to get us any supper.'

'Oh please, pretty please. Mum's left cottage pie to be heated up, and even I can boil a few peas. Come on, before it gets dark.'

'Once down the lane and back. No more.'

Daisy danced an exaggerated jig of triumph and ran round to the driver's side of the car. David sat beside her, one hand on the hand-brake as the car jerked out of the gate onto the lane. Fortunately Daisy seemed to have a natural ability to co-ordinate her hands and feet, so creeping along in first, then second, gear she drove the hundred metres or so to the point where the lane joined a wider country road.

'Let me go on,' she asked, turning onto the road without waiting for a reply.

'No!' David knocked the car out of gear and pulled on the handbrake.

'I'm not moving,' said Daisy obstinately. David reached across and took out the ignition key.

'Fine. I'll go home and eat the pie then,' he said. Daisy still had the power to amuse him when she pulled her round face into a fierce frown. He set off towards the house. Daisy waited for a moment or two, then got out of the car and trotted after him. As soon as she reached his side David turned back and with his longer legs had reached the car and dived into the driver's seat almost before she had turned. Laughing he drove past, up to the front door of the house and locked the car securely before going in.

Daisy put on a cheerful face, helped in the kitchen and after supper did most of her homework with his help.

If David had been more suspicious he would have wondered why Daisy was a model of good behaviour for the rest of the evening, went to bed rather early and apparently without even a glance at her television or computer. Tired himself, David was sound asleep well before midnight. Daisy waited until half an hour had passed since she heard the creak of the stairs, then she crept into David's room and listened to his quiet breathing for a minute or two. He was a heavy sleeper, she knew, and his bedroom was on the back of the house. There was little possibility of his hearing the car start up, and even if he did she would be away before he could follow. The car key was on the table beside his bed. She stealthily picked it up and tiptoed out of the room.

Daisy intended only to drive to the end of the lane, turn onto the wider road which reached a small roundabout after about five hundred yards. Here she would go all the way round and come back home. David would not know what she had done, but she would have the satisfaction of having got her own way in spite of him.

'Driving's easy,' she told herself. The start was made easier for her as David had left the car facing down the drive towards the lane. It took a minute or two for her to find the light switch, then the beam suddenly looked so bright that she thought it must shine through the upstairs landing window towards David's bedroom. If she was going she must be quick.

After a slightly jumpy start Daisy proceeded carefully in first gear, out of the gate and towards the road. Second gear was her favourite she decided, as the car moved smoothly along. At the junction Daisy did not need to slow down as the road was empty in both directions, so she headed with increasing confidence towards the roundabout. Before she got to it, she tried the movement that would put the car into third gear, clashed noisily at first, then succeeded. Immediately, the slow speed made the car start to judder, and Daisy instinctively accelerated a little to regain the smooth forward motion. She was at the roundabout before she realised. Panicked by the speed at which the car lurched past the first exit, she lost her bearings, saw what she thought was the way back towards home and shot off down the slip road onto the main eastbound road, a six lane dual carriageway.

Fortunately at this time of night there was less traffic than in the daytime, but the road was by no means empty. Barely in control Daisy drove off the slip road onto the inside lane just far enough in front of a huge truck heading for Felixstowe, but close enough to provoke a terrifying blast from its massive horn. By now shaking and sobbing, her hands slippery with sweat on the steering wheel, she lifted her foot from the accelerator and the truck swerved past her into the path of another. Both roared by with a cacophony of sound.

Now the road behind her was dark. Daisy was tempted to stop, calm down and think what to do next. But the empty blackness of the road, and a fear that if she stopped she may not be able to start the car again kept her moving. For a moment she wondered if she should leave the car and somehow walk home, but she no longer really knew where she was, or how far she would have to walk.

Ahead she saw a sign announcing the next junction. If she left the big road here and turned left, surely she would end up back where she started, she thought. At the top of this slip road to her relief a signpost showed the direction to a place she knew. Still in third gear, the car began juddering again as the speed dropped. This time Daisy had the presence of mind to change down into second, and decided to stay there no matter how slowly she had to proceed. Luckily, at this modest speed another left turn showed her that this was the way back towards her home village, and she suddenly recognised the road as being the one her mother would drive along on the way to the supermarket in town.

Unaware that she had the lights on high beam, Daisy could see ahead quite clearly and relaxed a little. The road was narrow, with trees and high hedges on each side, but with each minute she became more confident that she was close to home. After a long right hand bend there would be a left turning onto the home lane, then a quarter mile or so to the drive up to the house. Daisy became more confident and once again changed carefully into third gear.

Suddenly, as the car emerged from the bend, Daisy was confronted by a confusion of lights. There was an impression of red, a deafening roar and a blinding white light that filled her vision then flashed behind her as quickly as it had come. Instinctively ducking away from it, Daisy jerked the steering wheel. A horrible grinding impact dragged along the side of the car next to her.

151

As the car juddered almost to a halt Daisy accidentally trod on the accelerator instead of the brake and surged forward again. Her teeth clamped onto the side of her tongue but she hardly noticed the pain. Every muscle in her body was rigid with tension, and a strange choking scream burst from her lungs with every exhaled breath. Amazingly, the rest of the journey continued without mishap. She wrenched the wheel round to steer into the drive, took her feet away from the pedals, the car lurched and stalled, and silence fell around her.

A moment later the front door banged open and there was David, fully dressed, marching out towards her. He seemed not to notice the ominous clunk as he heaved the door open and dragged Daisy out. She was trembling so violently that she slid to the ground at his feet. This did not evoke any sympathy however. He pulled her to her feet and held her upright with two fistsful of her jersey, his face an inch from hers.

'What the fuck are you doing, you little idiot?' he yelled.

'I'm sorry, I didn't mean it,' Daisy wailed. 'I only was going to the roundabout and it went wrong.'

'You've been gone twenty minutes. I heard you go. Where've you been for twenty minutes, for God's sake?'

He didn't wait for her to reply, but pushed her vigorously ahead of him into the house.

Daisy was crying in earnest by now, great blobs of tears dripping from her chin. David followed her into the kitchen, saying nothing until he had put a glass of water in front of her and a wad of paper towel into her hand.

'What does 'it went wrong' mean?' he demanded.

'I meant to just go to the little roundabout and come back, but the car went fast and it went down on the main road.'

'What!'

'Then I drove off it again, and came back along that road to town where the woods are.'

'But why did you go in the first place?'

'It's your fault,' Daisy burst out. 'You wouldn't let me. If you'd let me drive a bit further before, I wouldn't have had to.'

'God, you've got a nerve, Daisy. It's my car and you are fourteen years old. You think you can do whatever you want, you stupid, spoiled child.'

'It's still your fault,' Daisy sulked. 'Anyway, the car might have bumped on something.'

'What d'you mean? Bumped?'

'There was a light, and I couldn't see properly and there was a scraping noise.'

'A red light? On the back road?'

'Yes. Well some of the light was red.'

'Road works. I came past there on the way here tonight. How bad is it?'

'I don't know. You dragged me in here before I had time to have a look.'

At that moment the door bell rang, long and loud. They both jumped and Daisy screamed. Through the glass of the front door a turning blue light was visible.

'Oh God,' said David. 'Get upstairs and stay there. And I mean, stay there.'

Daisy scuttled to the stairs and ran up as David waited to open the door. At the top she lay on the landing and peeped down through the banisters.

There were two police officers at the door.

'David Baines?'

'Yes, that's me.'

'This is your car?'

'Yes, and I know I may have caused a bit of damage to the barrier round the road works tonight. There didn't seem to be much point in stopping to report it there and then. I was going to do it in the morning.'

At the top of the stairs Daisy's heart began to race. David had moved aside and one of the officers stepped into the hallway. He produced a breathalyser and instructed David to blow into it.

The result was of course clear.

'You got here very quickly,' said David, sounding to Daisy remarkably calm. She could hear a pulse in her ears and she was breathing rapidly.

'The motorcyclist took your number and happened to meet us in the town centre. The car is registered to this address. I assume this is your home.'

David shrugged. 'Yes. It's my parents' home. Mostly I stay over with my girlfriend in Clarence Court, but yes, this is my home.'

'And you are here tonight. Why?'

'My parents are away, and I'm looking after my little sister. She's asleep.'

'So how old is she? Old enough for you to go out in the middle of the night?'

'Well, yes. She's fourteen and I was only out for a few minutes. I thought the shop at the service station stayed open all night, but it was shut. I went for cigarettes.'

Daisy shook her head. 'You don't smoke,' she whispered to herself. But what other reason could he have thought of, she wondered.

David asked, 'You mentioned a motor cyclist.'

'Yes, the one you nearly hit as you went through the red light.'

'I don't think so,' answered David. 'He came towards the lights so fast that he couldn't have seen whether I had stopped or not.'

The second officer reappeared at the door. 'Have you seen the damage to your car, mate?' he asked.

'Not properly. Again I thought that could wait until the morning.'

'You'll need to produce your driver's licence.'

'It's in the car, with the insurance certificate too.'

The second officer sounded almost friendly. 'Okay, let's see that now. I've got a torch here. I'll show you what you've done to your offside wing.'

David and the officer disappeared outside, leaving the first one standing inside the door, talking quietly into his radio. Daisy scuttled down the stairs.

'Don't blame David, please,' she whispered urgently. 'I don't want him to go to prison. It was me. I drove the car. It was scary. I didn't mean to hit anything.'

The policeman looked down at her. 'What d'you mean, it was you.?'

'I was driving. It was an accident. I never meant to do it.'

'You're the sister, are you?'

'Yes. David wouldn't let me drive, but I did. I'm sorry. Don't make him go to prison.'

'He's not going to prison. The car is taxed and insured, the motor cyclist probably was going too fast, I'm sure his licence is okay, he hasn't been drinking. The only damage he's done is to his own car. The barrier he knocked over isn't damaged. He isn't going to prison.'

Daisy thought for a moment. 'Are you sure?'

'Yep.'

'And you won't report him or anything?'

'We have to put in a report, but it won't go any further.'

'So I don't need to take the blame?'

There was an ominous silence as the officer looked at Daisy and frowned. 'You're dressed,' he said.

'I…er.. I heard you coming.'

He paused again, his expression hardening. 'Your brother said he was driving. If it was you, matters would be different. Either you took the car with his permission, in which case he would be in trouble, or you took it without his permission, and it's you that's in bother. So which is it?'

Daisy's mind whirled. Her momentary instinct to save David had been a mistake, she realised. She could actually be blamed, have to take the consequence. This time, unless she backed off immediately, it would go badly. As usual she was going to allow her brother to make life easy for her.

'Yes, I see,' she replied. 'It was just… if you thought it was me, it would be alright, because I'm just a kid. I thought you would believe me and I would be let off.'

'So it wasn't you?'

'No.'

He turned away, paused then turned back to her.

'I'm giving you the benefit of the doubt,' he said, 'because I don't think your brother deserves to be in trouble. But if what you said is the truth, and if he is taking the blame for you…'

'I know.' Daisy had regained her composure. 'You would think I was very spoiled.' She giggled.

'That's an easy word to use when you don't think about what it means. Spoiled… are you? Are you really spoiled?'

Daisy stared up at him. For the first time the word had meaning. Her eyes filled with tears.

Downfall

How many of us are as fortunate as Mr. Tweddle? From the day he stepped into his first school at the age of five, he knew he was in the right place. He enjoyed the company of other children, regarded teachers as people who existed to help him, and his work as interesting puzzles to be solved. He was clever enough without being a swot, sporty enough without being annoyingly competitive, pleasant looking with out being challengingly handsome. He took some teasing on account of his mop of ginger curls, but didn't bear grudges. He fitted in, and never saw a reason to explore a different environment.

Admittedly, for a while after he was appointed as headteacher of Mudford Magna primary school he wondered whether his elevated status had removed him from the fun of the classroom, then he realised he now had a whole school to play with.

On this particular morning he was humming 'The Sun has got his Hat on' while he opened some packages that had just been delivered. There was a knock on his door and a tousled head peeped round it about half way up.

'Good morning Tom Tom. Come right in.'

'You always say that Mr. T. I'm Tom. Tom tom is a drum.' The child rolled his eyes in mock exasperation.

'Well, I'll have to take care not to beat you then, won't I!'

'I told my Mum you said that and she said go right ahead it'll save her the bother. Why do my Mum and Dad call you McVitie?'

'Can't imagine,' said Mr. Tweddle, running his fingers through his ginger curls.

Mr. Tweddle opened the next box. 'Here, hold this,' he said, passing over one end of a string of bunting composed of the flags of European countries. Between them they stretched it across the room.

'How many of these do you know?'

Tom looked along the strip. 'That's England, and that one's Scotland 'cos my granddad supports them in rugby. And that one is all of them in the Union Jack, but I don't know any more.'

'What about this one? If you know about rugby you must have seen this.'

'Is it New Zealand?'

'No. Guess again.'

'Is it South Africa?'

'No, it's Wales.'

'Why does it have a dragon on it, then?'

'Some long ago Welsh king had a dragon on his flag and they've kept it ever since.'

'Why don't they have whales on it? They don't live in a place called Dragon.'

'Ah, I think we might have to have a lesson soon about words that sound the same but mean different things. Like… a bow that you shoot an arrow with, and a bow that you tie with your shoe lace. Or peace that's not war, and a piece of pie.'

Tom thought hard and giggled. 'Like pea and pee.'

Mr. Tweddle grinned. 'You've got the idea. But you didn't come here to exchange banter with me. What's up?'

'Miss Burney sent me to ask for printer ink.'

Mr. Tweddle went to the cupboard. 'Okay, I'll bring it because I've got some new coloured card for her class too. You scoot.'

In the stock cupboard, piling up necessities and art materials for the Upper Infants, he remembered that he had neglected to open an envelope that had come from his Chairman of Governors. The fact of it didn't matter, as he knew it contained the Minutes of a recent meeting, which he had already seen as an email. But the Chairman, Colonel F.G.W. Manners (ret'd) was old-fashioned and required all communication to exist on paper.

Mr. Tweddle thought of his Board of Governors and sighed. It seemed impossible to recruit younger members of the community, most of whom commuted a long way into Birmingham, and valued their evenings in front of the TV. Even the teacher member of the Board was the oldest member of staff, amiable Fred Potter, already with half his attention on retirement. Each of the others had an agenda of their own. The vicar, who had been ordained after retiring from work in a bank, was involving herself in local activities in the hope of boosting her tiny congregation. George the pub landlord, whose unshakeable view of the ideal school was rooted in his own experience of forty years before, believed that his link with the school identified his pub as being family friendly. Mrs. Grimshaw, wife of a prosperous haulier, was working hard to establish herself as part of a social set that she felt appropriate to her husband's income. School governor, trustee of a local horse rescue charity and provider of church flowers was her repertoire of good works. The colonel's rank and address of Mugford House impressed her and she ardently agreed with all of his pronouncements. Only Tom Tom's dad, representing the parents, seemed to be whole-heartedly behind the notion that a happy school was a successful school, and he, the local emergency plumber, sent apologies more often than not.

Briefly remembering the colonel's letter, Mr. Tweddle made a mental note to reply by the end of the day, or risk being regarded as lacking discipline.

The Upper Infants were restless Mr. Tweddle found when he arrived at the classroom. Miss Burney was the newest and youngest member of staff, admirable in her devotion to her young charges, but in Mr. Tweddle's view a bit unimaginative, and rather too apt to cling to routine.

'Tell you what,' he said. 'Let's take them outside for ten minutes. It's the first fine day for a week and they need to run around. I'll bring my chequered flag and they can run races.'

Outside, the flag was given to Miss Burney to wave and the children divided into groups to race towards her, running, or hopping, or hand in hand. It was a sunny, cool Spring day, and they all joined in with a will. After fifteen minutes, Mr. Tweddle called time. 'Just one more race, and this time I'll join in and beat you all.'

'That's not fair,' they chorused. 'You're big, you're a grownup. It's not fair.'

'Tell you what. I'll run backwards.'

It is quite difficult to beat a determined six-year-old over a short distance, so by the time Mr. Tweddle approached Miss Burney and the chequered flag, trotting backwards, most of the children were waiting for him.

'Wave the flag. Wave the flag,' they cried, and she stepped forward to do so just as he changed direction, cannoned into her, and they fell to the ground in a tangle of limbs. Miss Burney jumped up quickly, retrieved her dignity and declared the race over. Mr. Tweddle made the most of the situation, lying on his back, waving his arms and legs and calling 'Help, help,' until a crowd of giggling children were pushing and pulling him to get up. Order restored, Mr. Tweddle's natural authority came into play. 'Two lines, side by side. Walk in, in silence, following Miss Burney, and sit in your quiet corner'. Instant obedience ensued.

Sally Williams, whose best friend was absent with a rash, so had no partner, fell in beside Mr. Tweddle.

'Do you like Miss Burney?' she asked. 'I don't.'

'That's a shame. Of course I like her. What's gone wrong for you?'

'She won't let me bring my rat. I told her it's a nice rat, but she still said no. She said lots of people don't like rats.'

Mr. Tweddle ruffled his ginger curls. 'Miss Burney could be right though. What if you brought the rat and the other kids screamed and frightened it?'

'That would be bad.'

'So you leave the rat at home, and try to like Miss Burney. Okay?'

'If you do.'

'Yes I do, and I think you should.'

Sure enough, the Upper Infants were pacified, and listened to their story quietly, some with thumbs in their mouths.

'Thank you,' said Miss Burney. 'Do you think we should do this project I've been reading about, of getting the kids to run for a few minutes every day?'

'Why not? Can only be good for them. In fact we'll get all the infants doing it. I'll leave it to you to organise it. Tell the other staff I've agreed.'

As he wafted the chequered flag back into the cupboard, Mr. Tweddle failed to notice Colonel Manners' envelope drifting off the desktop and under the bookcase, there to remain, forgotten.

The term went on, mostly fun and pleasure for Mr. Tweddle, the few problems being met with good nature and humour. Life was calm at Mudford Magna Primary School.

Towards the end of term preparations were made for the most important Open Evening, when current and prospective parents came to admire the pleasant tidy building, the outdoor space, the displays of attractive work, and to meet the team; teachers, secretary, cooks, Mr. Tweddle and the Chairman of Governors. Many of the children were involved, as hosts or singing in the choir, or taking part n demonstration lessons. Test results were good again, justifying the school's motto, A Happy Child is a Successful Child.

Mr. Tweddle, proud of his school, relaxed and sociable with parents, enjoyed these occasions. After the speeches, the singing and the distribution of tea and biscuits, he ambled from room to room, chatting, self-effacingly receiving compliments, passing on praise to his staff. So he was surprised when Miss Burney, her face pale and anxious, appeared at his side and whispered, 'Colonel Manners told me to send you to my classroom immediately.'

'Oh, what's rattled him, then?'

'He said, straightaway, and he would tell you. He's cross!'

In the Upper Infants classroom he found Colonel Manners frowningly examining a display of artwork. The Infants had been asked to illustrate the things they had enjoyed during the term, and as Mr. Tweddle approached the colonel jabbed a finger at a large and colourful sheet mostly covered in blue and green paint. A set of goal posts at one side identified it as the playing field.

'What is your explanation for this being on open display in a classroom?' the colonel asked loudly.

Mr. Tweddle looked more closely. The name of Sally Williams was on a white label at the top. On the green area of the picture could be seen two recognisably human figures, lying flat, with the scribbled orange curls of one apparently between the thighs of the other. Alone the bottom in wavery infant handwriting was the caption

'Mr. Twedl liks Miss Burney.'

Mr. Tweddle suppressed a giggle. 'Yes, it's a bit unfortunate I guess, but obviously Miss Burney was there when it happened. I don't suppose for a moment that she thought of it as being anything other than what it was.'

'So she has attempted to explain. I have stationed myself in this room to observe reactions, and I can tell you it has caused a great deal of disquiet. Far too much ribald laughter and raised eyebrows, I can assure you.'

'Really? In my experience parents aren't that daft. It's a spelling mistake.'

'I sincerely hope that it is! Even you wouldn't condone an accurate representation of that kind of activity between yourself and a member of your staff.'

'Just a minute. What do you mean, even me?'

'Exactly that. You have just told me that this is a school where blatant spelling mistakes are put on display for all the world to see.'

Mr. Tweddle was speechless.

The colonel went on. 'I intend to call a special governors' meeting, to instigate disciplinary proceedings. I can no longer tolerate your casual unprofessional attitude, ignoring important communications from your Chairman of governors, disporting yourself with small children, dressing as you do...' he gestured towards Mr. Tweddle's chinos and open-necked shirt, and marched briskly from the room.

Mr. Tweddle sighed and stared out of the window across the playing field. He thought of his board of governors and a feeling of dread grew in him.

'But this is what I am,' he thought. 'I can't be anything else.'

The Food of Love

Every summer Harriet's parents rented a large house with a swimming pool in France, sometimes in Burgundy, sometimes in Dordogne. The plan each time was to invite and entertain friends from England, with their families, and these invitations were taken up with enthusiasm. Harriet hated it. The adult friends took as much notice of her as did her parents, which was very little. Their children were usually horrible in Harriet's opinion, spending their time in noisy ball games in the grounds, splashing and screaming in the pool, or whining about being bored.

Her parents made it clear that they were disappointed by Harriet's lack of social graces. The family were vaguely aristocratic; a grandfather had been the third son of a baronet, a favourite of Queen Victoria. Title and money had gone in another direction, but Harriet's mother was very aware of her connections, and made sure her circle of acquaintance was equally aware. Fortunately Harriet's father was an astute businessman, and the lack of fortune in the family had been more than overcome by his efforts in the City. The summer house parties enhanced and cemented a number of useful relationships.

To escape, Harriet retreated to the kitchen, where local women were employed to cater for the party. In a pretence that they were living a French lifestyle, the instruction to the cooks was to produce local specialities, excluding of course such things as snails and gizzards. Harriet was happy in the kitchen. She enjoyed watching the preparations, the careful trimming of meats, shaping of vegetables, tasting of sauces. Sometimes she was given small tasks, and as her interest grew she recorded what she had observed in a fat notebook. As well as absorbing a great deal of information about regional cuisine, she learned a useful amount of colloquial French and the names of many ingredients.

Harriet never did learn to mingle with the guests, to employ gracious small talk, or to spot a useful connection. At the end of her education at her expensive girls' school she left with excellent results in only two subjects, Cookery and French. Still with no clear view of her future, and certainly without ambition, she persuaded her father to send her to Italy, to a language school in Florence, where she could learn Italian, and, her parents hoped, grow up a bit.

In Florence Harriet fell in love three times. The first time was with the language, and the second time was with soup. The food in the school was dull, and she soon felt that a rotating menu of four kinds of pasta, plus unvarying antipasti, did not excite her, so she began to seek out local restaurants that would offer a wider selection of dishes that she could add to her expanding notebook. Without access to the kitchens she would taste and think and guess. Longing to cook for herself she told her father that the remaining terms of her course did not include residence in the school, and used the allowance he sent to rent a tiny studio flat with a minute kitchen. The soup that she loved was an intensely flavoured clear broth with a very few slivers of colourful vegetables floating in it. It took a number of experiments to achieve the clarity of the liquid, a stock of white onion, celery and tiny turnips, with a little garlic and a hint of ginger, reduced, skimmed and filtered. There was something missing, and Harriet added and took away, lost in concentration. Eventually, after infusing a large bunch of parsley in the stock, leaving it in until the liquid cooled, then removing it, she felt she had arrived at the right depth of flavour. It just remained to add lightly steamed asparagus tips, a few slivers of grated carrot and half a dozen peas to each serving, for colour. The broth was everything.

With the limited resources of her tiny kitchen Harriet found that she most enjoyed dishes that were cooked mainly in a single pot. She referred to her earlier notes and the memory of the French kitchens to experiment with Bourguignon stews, dark and thick with intensely reduced red wine sauces, cassoulet using cheap cuts of pork because she could not afford the duck meat and giblets that had been ubiquitous in the Dordogne.

Of course, one of the great pleasures of cooking is to share the results, so the third time Harriet fell in love it was with a young man. There was a quiet square, a little off the beaten track, with a silent fountain in one corner. A few tourists wandered through on their way between Dante's monument and the Ponte Vecchio. Next to the dry fountain this young man had set up an easel and a folding chair, and was drawing pastel portraits of anyone who would sit down in front of him. Harriet sat close behind him on the stone rim of the fountain. At that moment he was drawing a sweet-faced teenaged girl while her boyfriend stood by smiling. The image was quickly caught, slightly flattering, Harriet thought, the dark eyes just a little larger, the lips slightly fuller. When it was finished the girl and boy exclaimed over it, clearly seeing it as a totally accurate representation. The boy dropped a twenty euro note into a box at the foot of the easel.

Immediately another sitter arrived, this time an elderly American woman persuaded onto the chair by her corpulent husband. Harriet felt nervous; the woman had the signs of considerable cosmetic surgery in her face, and when she smiled at the young artist her mouth and eyes pulled into a grotesque grimace.

'No,' said the young man, in accented but fluent English. 'I don't want you to smile. It is hard to keep it natural after a while, you know. The muscles get tired. I think you are more beautiful in repose.'

The woman nodded, obviously relieved. Harriet watched as the image grew on the paper, capturing a mood of tranquillity. She suddenly saw the woman as she would have been ten years ago, not young, but not distorted by surgery. Again the portrait was received with pleasure, but this time only a few coins dropped into the box.

The artist turned to Harriet. 'Have you been waiting your turn?' he asked in Italian, smiling. 'I think you have been wondering if I am good enough to capture your beauty.'

Harriet laughed. 'I think you can make everyone beautiful,' she replied. 'And I am watching, not waiting.'

'Sit on my chair then. It isn't good for people to think I have no customers. They like to watch then decide to sit.'

Harriet sat, and he sketched rapidly. 'You are English. Your Italian is quite good, but in need of some practice, so you can talk to me. Tell me all about you and what you are doing in Firenze.'

Harriet felt there was little to tell, explaining about the language school, her little apartment and the exploration of local cafes. His interested expression and sympathetic murmurs, however, meant that in the fifteen minutes spent drawing her portrait she had confided her uncertainty about where her life would go next, her discomfort with the expectations of her family.

The boy put down his pencils, turned an attractive image on the easel towards her, and said, 'I have finished for today. Come and meet my mother.'

Slightly startled, Harriet nevertheless followed. During ten minutes walk, she learned that his name was Gino, his mother was a widow living with her sister Isabella and brother-in-law Enzo in an apartment above the uncle's shop, where unusual items were sold to tourists. Uncle Enzo made boxes, from matchbox size to blanket boxes, from ancient panels rescued from ruined country houses, polishing and distressing them to the appearance of antiques. 'But he clearly tells that they are new,' said Gino seriously. Aunt Isabella and his mother made cushions from old brocade and dolls' clothes in a variety of period styles.

The warm welcome from Gino's family extended to inviting her to stay until the end of her course. Their everyday conversations meant that within those six months Harriet became fluent, and was able to accept Gino's marriage proposal in his own language.

For a while Harriet could not quite understand why Gino wanted them to return to England. Whether or not he was right to think he would have more opportunities to paint proper portraits she did not know. Other reasons arose from the importance he placed on family relationships.

'You can see,' he explained, 'that my family is good. I don't need to be with them all the time to know that they love me. My mother will miss me, yes, but she will know that I do not go away because I no longer care for her. My brother in Australia, he comes home once every year and it is as if he has not been gone. But your family, it is wrong, it does not work properly. If we stay here in Italy you will lose them for ever. I can't let you do that.'

Harriet allowed herself to be persuaded, though in her heart she felt that no amount of proximity would cause her parents to regard her as anything but a disappointment. Her view was confirmed when she told her parents that she intended to marry Gino.

'That's no more than I would have expected from you, Harriet. A pavement artist indeed.' Harriet's mother looked up briefly from her copy of Country Life.

'Gino isn't a pavement artist. Not how you mean, anyway. He's a portrait painter. It just happened that in Florence he made a good income working out of doors.'

Harriet knew this sounded feeble, but her mother's cool lack of interest was impossible to combat.

'Do as you wish. But don't expect Daddy to fork out for a proper wedding. Find your own register office. And don't imagine that any of the family will be there.' The magazine page was turned decisively.

Gino's mother, aunt and uncle and three cousins flew to England for the wedding. Ernesto, a more distant cousin owned and ran a small Tuscan-style restaurant in a Cotswold village, and a jolly family meal followed the ceremony. Gino kept glancing at Harriet, expecting to see that she was saddened by the absence of her own family. But Harriet was happy, relieved. The only expectation of her now was to be content with Gino, and that was easy.

Ernesto owned a small cottage near the restaurant which Gino and Harriet rented cheaply. Gino put some advertisements in the local country life-style magazines, and began to get some commissions to paint winsome children and plump brides. One subject asked to be painted sitting in his vintage sports car. Gino enjoyed that and a number of similar commissions followed, several being portraits of the car without the owner. He became resigned to the fact that his inability to make his subjects less than attractive and less than happy meant that he was unlikely to reach a different type of client.

'It's because you are a kind person,' Harriet told him, 'and that's why everyone loves you.' It was true that Gino's sunny nature invited affection; 'but not from my family' thought Harriet.

Her parents kept contact to a minimum. Gino resolutely insisted that he and Harriet visit every few weeks, but those times were awkward and, for Harriet, embarrassing.

'Wait until the babies come,' said Gino. 'Your mother will change then, I promise you.'

It was true that when their daughter Lucia was born Harriet's mother was quick to visit, but her first remark was a bland 'Well, she certainly resembles her father', and after that the normal lack of warmth and contact resumed.

For more than ten years Harriet, Gino and Lucia were contented in their simple life. Gino painted enough to support his small family. Harriet gave French and Italian conversation lessons, and cooked in the restaurant at lunchtimes. Her flair for improvisation she indulged at home, remembering the flavours of those French and Italian dishes she had enjoyed. Local markets and farm shops were a pleasure to her, where she bought unusual ingredients, experimented with combinations of taste and texture, jotting notes in the same way as she had done as a child. Sometimes she thought of writing her own recipe book, but part of the pleasure for her was in knowing that many a recipe contained a secret, an ingredient that would seem out of place to most people. She was quite amused when she read that Heston Blumenthal was making some of the same kind of experiments. Savoury ice creams and jelly that looked like worms were old hat to Harriet. Lucia, fortunately, had an adventurous nature when it came to eating and was a willing taster of her mother's concoctions.

Twice a year time was spent with Gino's Italian family, a week in Florence and a week with cousins near Viareggio, then Gino's mother visited them in England every year around Christmas time. Of course, Harriet came to feel that these were her true family; the duty visits to her parents continued, during which Gino was treated with cool politeness and Harriet more or less ignored. By the time she was ten Lucia refused to go.

Suddenly and horribly Gino became ill. At first he thought he was reacting badly to a new brand of oil paint that he was trying, as he felt sick and tired, and his head ached. He took a few days away from his paints, and stayed in bed complaining of strange pains that moved about his body stiffening his joints. Then when he got up one afternoon Harriet saw a huge purple bruise was spreading across his ribcage. A frightening memory came to Harriet of a girl in her school who died as a teenager. There was no delay on the part of their doctor, or in the hospital in Gloucester. Harriet's worst fear was true; Gino had an acute form of leukaemia.

The treatment was difficult, and in a short time the oncologist told them that it was not having the hoped-for effect. Gino was dying.

Harriet took him home. They wanted all of their remaining time to be together, and it was easier for Gino's mother who came with the determination to stay until the end. Harriet's parents sent a condolence card, one normally designed for a funeral, containing a brief note. 'Sorry to hear of your trouble'. Harriet threw it in the bin.

Gino's pain was controlled; he was tired and slept more and more, but one day he insisted that he and Harriet talk about his funeral arrangements. It was not really a discussion, as he had thought about what he wanted to say, and Harriet had only to listen and agree.

'Don't have a ceremony in church, Harriet,' he said. 'Go to the crematorium with Lucia and my mother. I want to be cremated, and we cannot afford the cost of anything more. Let it be as simple as possible. Promise me.'

Harriet nodded, the painful swelling of her throat preventing words.

Gino continued, 'But afterwards, there is something I want you to do. My family will come, I can't stop them, but they will not go to the crematorium. I want you to cook for them, a beautiful family meal, and talk about me and tell them how happy we have been.' Harriet nodded through her tears. 'But next,' he said, 'and this is important to me, don't give up with your parents. I don't understand them, and I think if I had been given another hundred years I never would. Treat them the same. Invite them and try to show them how family can be.'

Harriet opened her mouth to say that it would be hopeless, then stopped as Gino lay back exhausted. She would think of a way to honour the promise without exposing her Italian family to the hauteur of her parents.

The events passed almost as Gino wished. After his cremation Harriet waited a few days gathering her courage for facing all the relations. She had decided that she would feed everyone as lavishly as she could, but would keep the two sides of her family separate. Gino's mother, brother, Aunt Isabella, Uncle Enzo and three cousins gathered quietly at the restaurant with Ernesto. He had closed the restaurant for the day so that they could all be there together and Harriet busied herself in its kitchen. She prepared the favourite vegetable broth, simmering, tasting, infusing. Then she made a crust of apricots, ginger and shallots for two succulent racks of lamb. Asparagus and tender French beans were served generously coated in garlic flavoured butter. Fruits and cheeses and bowls of tiramisu were laid out on side tables. The family did as Gino wished and talked and wept happily recalling his childhood escapades, his fun with Lucia as a baby, the happy holidays in Italy.

Harriet was carried through on a wave of affection, bolstered by a hidden determination that she would indeed give her parents the same level of hospitality whether they wanted it or not. She had been mildly surprised that her mother had agreed coolly but readily to come to the cottage the next day.

'I suppose that now he is gone, you may find that you need your own family,' her mother had said. Harriet thought 'Don't try to get me to believe that all this time it's been me rejecting you,' and she realised that in all the years since she met him, her mother had never once addressed Gino by name.

Preparing for her parents, this time in her own kitchen, Harriet decided to evoke the rich meaty dishes of Burgundy and the ill-fated holidays of her childhood. Slow-cooked beef simmered in a thick sauce based on Pinot Noir wine, with tiny button mushrooms, whole shallots, crisply fried lardons and herbs from her garden. Then there were a few extra ingredients, her secrets as she thought of them, including a few pruneaux d'Agen, blended into a cupful of the wine, to give a richness and darker colour to the sauce. A tiny sprinkling of Cayenne pepper to add the interest of a hint of heat. Alongside this would be a dish of boulangere potatoes, crisp and golden to soak the rich sauce.

Lucia set the table, sulking a bit at the thought of greeting her unloved grandparents. Harriet had no intention of inflicting the meal on her daughter, and when the work was done she sent her off to join the Italian family all still gathered with Ernesto.

The parents arrived. Harriet made little effort to be sociable, ushering them straight to the table and leaving it to her father to pour wine from the bottle open in front of him. She assumed that her parents would ascribe her silence to grief, whereas in fact she was holding back her anger.

The stew was served, generous helpings to her parents, and a small amount for herself. Eating this in their presence was repugnant to her. As they ate, and congratulated her on the flavour, Harriet toyed with her small helping, raising a little to her lips, only to put it down again as she listened to her mother insincerely remarking that it was unfortunate that Harriet was widowed so young, but that with her culinary skills she could perhaps find herself working in a fashionable restaurant somewhere. A new chapter in life was opening up.

When the meal was over, Harriet stood up. She had prepared what she wished to say.

'Today is one event in the way Gino wished me to remember his life and acknowledge his passing,' she said. 'He particularly wanted me to spend this time with you, as family life was the most important thing for him. It is sad that you never wished to know him, as he was the kindest and most considerate man I have ever known. He had a great talent for making people feel happy about themselves through the way he depicted them in their portraits, and he gave me the security and self-confidence that comes from being deeply loved. As you go home now, and I mean now, I know you will be carrying a little of Gino with you.'

Followed somewhat hesitantly by her parents, Harriet raised her glass, smiling towards the beautifully carved box on the mantelpiece, made by Uncle Enzo to contain Gino's ashes, the quantity reduced now by the two tablespoonfuls that had gone into the boeuf bourguignon.

Fantasy

Betty isn't her real name. She is one of those actresses whose face everyone knows, without being exactly famous. If you saw her in the street, you would turn and look, and think 'I've seen her in something… what was it…?' and maybe an hour later it would come to you. So, I'll call her Betty, because you would also recognise her name though without linking it to the face. She has been fortunate in her career, very rarely without work, some leading parts in provincial theatre, lots of not quite starring roles in television drama. Her own measure of success is that she has never had to do a TV commercial. I can't fully understand why real fame has eluded her, because she is so talented. But I would think that; I'm her husband.

I've known Betty for a long time, and I know her as well as anyone could. For quite a while after we met I thought she was a really complex character, difficult to pin down, impossible to understand. Then I realised a simple basic fact about her. Betty was a liar. She lied with skill, imagination, enjoyment. Her lies were so frequent, sometimes so trivial that you might have thought it was an obsession. But it was not; it was too deliberate for that. Betty lied as a kind of hobby, a skill that she enjoyed exercising, improving. It was fun!

We talked about this, Betty and me, because like most people I think it matters. Betty didn't. She said she did no harm, and to be honest I can't think of a time when she seriously hurt anyone with her 'imaginings' as she preferred to call them. There was a sort of innocence about her, which was quite appealing. In any case she blamed her mother, but in an affectionate way.

Betty claims to remember her first lie. The timing is right, as there is a certain amount of research that says children learn to lie at about the age of two and a half. She may have remembered, but it could be that she absorbed the story, as it was frequently told as a kind of indulgent family joke. Apparently, when she was a toddler she was given as a present a big box of wax crayons. She described to me the colours, the soft waxy smell of them, the paper tube that surrounded each one and held it together even when the wax itself had snapped. Immediately there was the urge to use them, to spread and blend the vivid yellow, ominous purple, mouth-watering green. The best place for this was on the cream wall of the dining room, where she had been left for a few minutes sitting up at the table with a large piece of boring paper in front of her. In a short time an area of the wall was satisfyingly adorned with a burst of colours.

In came Betty's mother, Lilian. 'Betty! Did you do that?' Foolish question! No one else was there, no one else possessed a big box of beautiful crayons.

'No,' replied Betty. 'Umpy Dumpy did it.'

'Umpy Dumpy?'

In exactly the rhythm of the nursery rhyme Betty answered, 'Umpy Dumpy drawed on the wall.'

Lilian was not a disciplinarian; in fact some thought the standard of behaviour she demanded of her children was lax to the point of non-existence. She burst out laughing, whirled Betty into her arms and danced around the room singing, 'Humpty Dumpty drawed on the wall, Betty's an artist I don't care at all.' Betty laughed too, her sweet little face pressed to her mother's smiling cheek.

The dining room had a panelled wainscot and Betty's piece of art work was enclosed within one panel. Far from being removed, it was embellished. Lilian took a fine brush and a small tin of gold paint and transformed the surround into a kind of rococo frame. There it stayed for several years, until Betty began to be a little embarrassed by the humorous reverence with which her juvenile work was introduced to visitors.

Another lie which Betty remembered as having received parental approval happened when she was perhaps four years old. Someone had given Lilian a box of lovely exclusive chocolates which she left open on the kitchen table. She said that a few chocolates eaten now and then in passing did not have the moral burden of those eaten while sitting on the settee with one's feet up and a light-hearted magazine on one's lap. Naturally, Betty, being as fond of chocolates as her mother but with less willpower, found the box and ate quite a few within the space of a couple of minutes. Discovered *in flagrante* and with chocolate in evidence around her lips, she was asked, 'Betty, have you eaten my chocolates?' Did Lilian ever learn not to ask a question to which the answer is clearly known?

'No,' answered Betty. 'A bird flew in the window and took them.'

'A bird? Took four chocolates?'

'I 'spect it has little children birds what like chocolate.'

'But it must have been a very big bird to carry four chocolates all at once.'

'It was a *very* big bird, with a big, big golden beak and big claws, and it took one chocolate in its beak and two in its claws.'

'That's three. What happened to number four?'

'Well… it came again for another one.'

'And the chocolate that is on your face. Where did that come from?'

Betty licked around her mouth speculatively. 'Well I snatched one off it to save it and it must have accidentally gone on my cheek.'

'Did the bird close the window after itself, then?' asked Lilian indicating the closed window.

'Don't be silly. Birds can't do that. I closed it to stop it from coming back.'

Lilian picked her daughter up and started to wipe her face with the dishcloth. This soon turned into a game of struggling, tickling and laughter.

'Well, little monkey,' said Lilian, depositing her daughter on the floor. 'You've certainly got a good imagination. Would you like a chocolate as a reward for your effort against the enormous bird?'

'Yes please,' replied Betty although she felt a bit sick.

A bit later Betty was with her father. 'Daddy what is a magination?'

'Why do you ask?' he answered cautiously, aware that conversations with Betty were not always straightforward.

'Well, Mummy says I've got one.'

'Okay, usually a person with an imagination can make up good stories.'

'Is it good to have a magination?'

'I think so, as long as they are nice stories.'

Betty nodded thoughtfully.

By this time Betty had a little brother, whom she was encouraged to love dearly. His name was John, but everyone called him Baby. Sometimes she did love him, sometimes she wanted to smack him. Until he could talk, smacks that were given when no one was looking caused a wail that Betty convincingly described as the result of biting his own finger, or seeing a scary spider which had run away, or maybe having a pain in his tummy. Generally Betty was given the benefit of the doubt when presenting these reasons, but the first time Baby was able to say 'Betty smack,' she realised that she had to torment him in other ways.

Now Betty's acting skills came to the fore. Baby loved stories, and Betty, able to read well by the age of seven or eight, was given the task of entertaining Baby at bedtime from the many books that were in the children's bedroom. Poor Baby couldn't escape as he shared a room with his big sister.

Betty's first success in acting out the story for Baby came with *Where the Wild Things Are*. This delightful book gave her plenty of scope for growling, showing fierce teeth and grotesque faces. Baby was thoroughly scared in an enjoyable sort of way, and at the end of the story Betty would cuddle him and soothe him so that he learned to look to her for warmth and reassurance. After a while Betty gave up on books and relied on her own imagination, which was indeed good. Baby would be regaled with tales of strange creatures outside the bedroom window that were more fearsome if you could not see them. She would stalk round the room with clawed hands hissing dreadful spells, invoking witches and wolves, pretending to hear mysterious footsteps on the landing or scratching above the ceiling. Baby, wide-eyed and trembling deliciously would eventually leap onto Betty's bed to be comforted and told he was safe with her.

'Tell me more,' he would beg, sticking his thumb in his mouth and dropping asleep to the ideas of giant crabs crawling up a beach, snakes slithering through the undergrowth towards the swings in the park where Lilian and Daddy took him on Saturdays. The result of this upbringing has been that Baby was, and is, Betty's greatest fan, telling people proudly that even as a small child she was able to conjure a different world with the power of her words and actions.

In school, many more opportunities arose for Betty's inventiveness to come to her aid. This was when I met her. Aged seventeen, I found myself sitting next to her in an A-level English lesson. Miss Rutter our teacher was collecting in homework essays. When it came to Betty's turn to hand hers over she adopted an expression of deep contrition.

'I'm so sorry, Miss Rutter. I don't actually have it to hand in. I accidentally left my bag on the bus.' As she said this she kicked my ankle and with a rapidly down-turned eye indicated that I should surreptitiously push her school bag out of sight.

'That was careless Betty,' said the teacher, 'but apparently you have retrieved the bag as I can see it on the floor next to Dan's feet.'

'You see, it was a bit of a good turn that went wrong. I was on the bus and it came to the stop at the end of the Precinct. I looked out of the window, and I saw an old lady sitting in the bus shelter just trying to get up, and the driver took no notice and he drove on. I was so mad! But I knew there were traffic lights just there so I jumped up and ran to the front and told the driver to stop and open the door.'

'I'd be surprised if he did. They shouldn't let people get on and off between stops.'

'Well he wouldn't, then I told him I was going to be sick so he did open the door. I thought I could sort of hang out, like, gagging a bit, until she came. But she was walking so slowly. I jumped down to tell her to hurry and he drove off.'

'So that's how the bag was lost.'

'Yes, but I wasn't worried, because I had been sitting next to Dan, and I knew he would rescue it and bring it in this morning.' Here she gave me a sort of coy smile and the hint of a wink that made me feel like some kind of hero, even though I knew that stuff was a lie. I always walked home, and in any case I was playing football after school yesterday.

'Well, Betty. I suppose I have to applaud your attempt to do a good deed. But I still need to see your essay.'

'I've done most of it, Miss. And I've got the notes. I'll do it at lunchtime.'

As it happened she and two of her friends sat nearby in the canteen. I ate slowly, hoping they would speak to me, as I didn't know anyone else at that time. I was new to that school; the one I was at before didn't have a sixth form. But eventually I realised I would have to make the first move. The three of them had been sitting for ages, chattering and sharing a bottle of Coke.

'Shouldn't you be doing your essay somewhere?' I asked, regretting as I spoke the accusatory tone of my voice.

Betty looked up at me, her large dark eyes brimming with tears. 'I just don't feel up to it', she said, her voice roughened by emotion. 'The old lady fell when I made her hurry for the bus, and I've just heard that she has died.'

'Oh God, that's awful. Who told you? I didn't realise that you knew her.'

'Course I did. She was my Granny's neighbour. That's why I wanted to rescue her.' She was openly weeping now. I made a sort of gesture towards comforting her, and in so doing saw that her two friends were convulsed with laughter behind her.

'What's up with them?' I asked indignantly. Betty turned away, her shoulders shaking.

'You really went for it, didn't you!' grinned one of the girls. 'She said you would be a right softie.'

'You mean..?' I turned back to Betty who was wiping her eyes.

'Yeah, well... not very good taste, but it was a joke. I knew I could make you believe me. Even when I said I was with you on the bus, you wanted to believe me, didn't you.'

It was true, even in that moment when I knew she was making it up, the conspiratorial smile and wink had made me want to be on her side. I shrugged and tried to look cool about it.

'Still, what about the essay? How're you going to get away with that?'

'Oh I'd done it. Could have handed it in this morning but this was more interesting.'

The other girl said. 'It's her hobby, like. Target, one a day taken in. But today, double duds. You and Miss Rutter in one go.'

'What's the point?' I asked Betty.

'Like she said. It's fun. Doesn't do any harm.'

I suppose I could have argued the point, but I didn't want to. I was intrigued, and wanted to know her better. Fancied her as well of course, along with half the rest of the lads in the sixth form. At the time I couldn't have explained what made her so attractive. Her face was neat, with regular unremarkable features, her figure almost boyish. She was clever and athletic, and somehow dangerous. Except for the two friends, Clare and Wendy, girls didn't like her much. She was manipulative, there was no doubt, and unpredictable, and I suppose girls aren't interested in that kind of challenge in a friend.

Clare and Wendy thought she was funny, and their laughter kept them safe.

That was how I met Betty, and somehow she became a fixture in my life. I didn't really want to shake her off, because I was in love with her in that inexplicable way that overcomes irritation, bafflement about her behaviour, and long absences. Also, she didn't seem to want to be shaken off. All through the time that I was at university and then law school, and she was a drama student in London, she would turn up from time to time, amuse me, sleep with me, then disappear for weeks. She would never say that she loved me, but swore that there was no other man in her life, and that she couldn't do without me. The school friend Clare was doing the same course as I was, and she told me that as far as she knew, Betty was telling me the truth about that. For the time being I was satisfied, though I lied a bit to Betty myself, about other girls. Betty seemed a very unreliable basket for all my eggs, if you see what I mean.

After I qualified, I got a surprisingly lucrative job as an in-house lawyer with a London investment bank. Betty had been a year or two out of drama school and, as I said before, was working quite regularly. She had an attractive voice and a talent for local accents, so for a while she concentrated on work for BBC radio. She was taken on by an agency with links to a number of TV production companies. Like many actors she claimed only to truly love the stage and a live audience. Never one to turn down work she trotted off all over the place no matter how small a part to fulfil this need. A summer season play in Southwold, a pantomime in Nottingham, a miserable Ibsen in Newcastle. But London was her base, and usually that meant with me. I was happy for her to turn up unannounced, less so when I knew she was in town but wouldn't tell me where.

When I was twenty seven and well-established in my extremely well-paid job, I had a stroke of financial luck, in the form of a substantial legacy from a childless godmother. It enabled me to put down a hefty deposit on a long lease of a large flat in Camden, not far from the canal. It was the ground floor and semi-basement of the end of one of those ubiquitous terraces. Unusually the front door of the house led only onto the staircase for the upper floors. My entrance was through a gate into the garden, also mine, from a quiet side street, which gave it great privacy. I lived there for almost a year without even seeing the people who occupied the rest of the house. I loved it. There was a large living area from the front to the back of the house, with a small ultra-modern kitchen at the garden end of it. On the lower floor were two bedrooms, the bathroom and a large windowless store room. The mortgage was pretty steep, but I could afford it. By coincidence friend Clare, now a junior solicitor with a big London firm, was two streets away, so when Betty's absence involved Clare's sofa, I would be told. At that time I was irritated, but Clare was worried. She was quicker than I was to see that Betty was asking for trouble.

As I said, Betty spent a lot of time with me when she was in London. She had become a member of a touring company putting on contemporary plays in non-theatre venues throughout the south east. So one night they could be in a village hall in deepest Kent then the next day performing a matinee in an East End comprehensive school. Having a home with me was very convenient for Betty, but still she went on unexplained walkabouts for a night or two. 'To keep my independence.' she said.

For instance, one Monday morning, having stayed in my flat for three weeks, she waved cheerily at the garden door. 'See you soon, Danny boy.'

'I wish you wouldn't call me that. Where are you going?' I could ask that kind of question with no anticipation of an honest answer.

'Mrs. Mason. I haven't seen her in a while.' Mrs. Mason was a widow who lived in a pleasant mansion flat up the Finchley Road. Betty had lodged with her for a few months when she was at drama school, and they had kept in touch.

'Hang on, you spent the weekend with her just last month. Didn't you?'

'Oh I can't remember.' She was gone.

I must admit, on that occasion I followed her, and found she was telling the truth. The previous visit, I was not so sure. She had come back with a story about smoke alarms and fire engines and one old guy from another of the flats standing on the pavement wearing a long flowery nightdress.

On the whole this was a good time, and it lasted for almost two years. Betty and I were getting on for thirty; she still worked with the company a lot of the time, but was also doing quite a bit of TV work. That's about the time when you might have begun to see her as a familiar face without knowing her as a name. We were happy I think, but then I became more concerned about Betty's habit. Until that time most of the stories were funny, or outrageous, or pointless, without malice. Then a darker element crept in.

For example, Betty and the company had a four week engagement around Bristol, and she was staying with John, or Baby as she still called him. He phoned one day to tell me that he was worried about her because it seemed that she had a stalker. With a note of resignation in his voice he admitted that it could be one of her stories, but he couldn't take the risk. He knew I was going over to visit that weekend and would I look after her as he had plans that couldn't include taking her to wherever she was working and collecting her after every performance.

'Is that what you have been doing?' I asked.

'I want to, but often she won't let me. She just skips off without telling me. You know what she's like.'

'So what has she told you about this stalker?'

'It's a man who spoke to her on the bus. She says he waits for her and follows her but doesn't speak. She knows he is following her because of course she going to different places, church halls and schools and so on, and he's always there. She says he's harmless and she's quite flattered, but I think that's stupid.'

'Yeah, well so it is. I'll talk to her, and to him if he exists.'

So that weekend I waited for the story. Sure enough it came out, but she knew better than to try to take me in. No, the joke was on Baby.

'He is so gullible. You'd think by now he would know when I'm kidding him, wouldn't you,' Betty laughed.

'There's no stalker then?'

'Of course not. I just improved the truth a bit.'

'How?'

'Well, this young guy was sitting next to me on the bus, and he said, You're in Holby aren't you? I saw you in last night's episode. So I said yes, but he was very observant because it was one time when I was just sitting up in bed in a hospital ward with two doctors arguing over me. It wasn't a speaking part. So he said he'd noticed because he thought I looked like Amanda Holden and he was a big fan of hers. So I said Amanda Holden is years older than I am, and he scowled and got off the bus. Never saw him again, but Baby gives me a lift to places because he thinks I'm going to be abducted.'

Of course I told her that a story like that was stupid and dangerous.

'What really bothers me is that one day something horrible will happen to you, and no-one will believe you. A real stalker for instance.'

'Oh, don't go on. There's no harm in it.'

At least she accepted that it was perhaps unkind to John, who had a lifetime of being taken in by her stories. She apologised to him for 'exaggerating a bit', but I don't think it really made any difference to her attitude.

'Why do you need for John to worry about you? It doesn't help you and it must be horrible for him.'

Betty shrugged. 'Shows he cares, I suppose,' she muttered in an offhand manner, clearly not wanting to continue the conversation. Sometimes it was impossible to pin her down so I let it go. It was then that I wondered if I should be concerned about her mental health. Betty had never been deprived of care and affection; rather the reverse as Lilian had always been indulgent, John admiring, and myself... well, endlessly patient I suppose. Had the stories become more dangerous after her father died while she was a student?

By this time Betty didn't usually bother to tell her stories to me. She knew that either I would see through them immediately or I would tell her that I didn't believe anything she said, which was tricky for her when she was telling me the truth. This didn't mean that I was immune to the consequences though. There were times when a story told to someone else could hurt or annoy, even when I knew it was fabrication. One occasion came after the Bristol job when she was taken on to cover a lead role in a long-running London play. She didn't expect it to amount to anything but an occasional matinee to give the star (a really big name) an afternoon off. But a week or two after Betty started, the star turned out to be pregnant and liable to 'morning' sickness all day. So Betty got to do the last six weeks of the run. She was brilliant, not trying to replicate the performance of the absent star, but making the part her own, and the reviews picked this up. She got terrific notices, including in the nationals.

I decided to give her a treat as she had done so well, so I took her to Paris for a few days. We had a great time, strolling arm in arm by the Seine, eating well, browsing fashion stores and bookshops, seeing Swan Lake at the Palais Garnier. I even asked her (again) to marry me. She laughed but didn't say no. For both of us it was the best relaxing time we had had together for ages.

When we got back to London the mood seemed to continue, then one evening shortly afterwards we met a drama school friend of hers in a bar.

'How's life?' he asked.

'Oh I've just had a professional disaster,' replied Betty.

'No you haven't. I saw you. You were great,' he said, referring to the play.

'That was okay, it was what happened afterwards,' she said, doing the big sad eyes thing. 'I had a phone call one day as I was walking to the theatre, not a brilliant signal, but a woman saying she was Mr. Spielberg's secretary, would I call him as he had seen my performance and was interested in crackle crackle crackle.' She made the scratchy noise of a phone signal breaking down.

'You're kidding. Actual Spielberg!'

'That was my reaction, but I'd got the number she said, so I phoned and it really was Mr. Spielberg's office in Los Angeles. I said, You mean Mr. Spielberg the film

211

producer? Yes, that's right. And he wants to speak to me? Yes, he is in the UK at the moment and he could meet you in Liverpool. Liverpool? I thought he would be in London. No, just now he is in Liverpool, getting the vibe for a production about the Beatles.'

The friend was open-mouthed, and, I could see, seething with jealousy.

'I don't believe it!' Ah so you know her quite well, I thought.

'Nor did I believe it at first,' said Betty with dramatic emphasis on '*at first*'. 'But I went to Liverpool, found his hotel, and I got there in time to be told that he had just died!'

'Steven Spielberg is dead!'

'That's just it. It wasn't Steven Spielberg, it was Arthur Spielberg. He makes TV commercials for men's grooming products.'

Of course, we all laughed, and it was over, just another of Betty's stories, possibly true, possibly not, as far as the friend was concerned. But I was angry and hurt out of proportion to the situation. Later, I said to Betty, 'Why couldn't you have just said that we had a lovely time in Paris. We'd just got back, feeling good, I thought, and

212

you have to start looking for admiration or sympathy or whatever that daft story was supposed to elicit.'

She shrugged. 'I don't know. What does it matter?'

'Well, I suppose a story like that doesn't matter. But when you worry John, when you won't be up front with me about where you're living, that's not fair. Why do you need to do that?'

Something in my attitude told Betty I wouldn't let her slide out this time.

'I guess I feel safer if I know someone cares about me.'

'But you know that anyway. Your mother, your brother, me. Clare; heaven knows you've told enough tales to her but she still phones me to ask if you are okay after you've spun her some yarn about being homeless or whatever.'

'I didn't!'

'Well that's how she heard it when you told her you'd slept on five sofas in a fortnight and hers was the comfiest.'

'Well, if she's a bit sorry for me I can sleep over at hers if I need company.'

'You can sleep over at mine if you need company.'

She tried a shaky grin. 'You keep asking to marry me. Clare doesn't.'

'Oh Betty. Could you just try to be truthful? Maybe a month, a week even.'

She stared at the floor. 'I don't know. It scares me. It feels like an addiction or something. I can't promise in case I can't keep it up.'

'What about professional help? A counsellor of some kind.'

'I'm not crazy Dan.' She began to cry. 'I will try. Give me a week or two, then I promise I'll talk about it again.'

I gave in; the tears were real. She didn't keep the promise to talk about it of course. I tried, even finding out where she could get counselling, but it just made her more upset.

After that I didn't see much of her for a couple of weeks. She was in Salford Quays recording a radio play for the BBC, then when she came back I had to go to Newcastle for a working week for a conference. I deliberately didn't ask where she would stay while she was back in London but I made sure she had her key for my flat. It was late November, and although she was only involved in some daytime rehearsals I had this almost parental need to know she would be safe at home after dark. There was no need for sofa-surfing and no-one there to propose to her. Ruefully, I thought if Betty's crazy, so am I a bit.

The last day of the conference, Friday, I was looking forward to getting home, and at the same time nervous that Betty would have gone walkabout. So once I was on the train I phoned Clare and asked her to check that Betty was home at the flat, which she did.

A couple of hours later, half an hour south of Peterborough, my phone rang. It was Clare. 'Dan, when you get back, come straight to mine. Betty is here and she's in a bit of a state.'

'Why? What's happened?' I could hear that Clare was trying hard to sound calm, and to keep her voice down.

'I don't know. I think it's some kind of breakdown. Or something terrible has happened. Some of what she's said is so bizarre.'

'What? Tell me what's happened.'

'I can't. She's saying she's been attacked in some way, but she isn't hurt. I'm really scared, Dan. I want to call an ambulance but she won't let me. She just keeps asking how long you will be.'

I looked at my watch. 'Tell her less than an hour. Depends on getting a cab straightaway, but I should be at Kings Cross in about twenty minutes.'

I sat back, concentrating on breathing slowly and thinking about just how bizarre Betty's story would be for Clare to sound so serious.

Well, this is how it came out, with Betty white-faced and shaking, hunched next to me on Clare's sofa, her arms gripped tightly round her bent legs. She got home to the flat, poured a glass of wine, Clare phoned to ask how the rehearsals were going, and she got a few things out of the fridge ready to make some supper. Just then, she heard the garden door open and assumed it was me arriving home. But it wasn't me, the house door opened with a crash, the kitchen light went out, and she could see just the silhouettes of four men coming in. They were marching in line, like weird soldiers, she said, and wearing strange helmets with visors. Within a second, they had seized her and put a cloth bag over her head. Then they held her tight and wound cling film around her body from neck to toe, so that she couldn't move, or see.

'Just a minute' I said. 'They put a bag on your head and actually wrapped you in cling film?'

'That's what it felt like. And you think you would scream, but when it happens you can't, you can't get it out, it's as if your throat is closed. And I couldn't breathe properly the bag was so thick.'

'But you could hear what they said?' asked Clare. 'What did they want? I guess the place has been trashed.'

'No they weren't burglars, and they said nothing the whole time. They just finished wrapping me up, then they lifted me so that I was carried over their heads and marched out, like a procession. I could hear their feet all stamping together. And in a moment they pushed me into a car, well I think more likely a van, because they just pushed me in and I lay flat. I tried to struggle but the cling film was so tight and wound round so many times that I couldn't move at all. My arms were pressed on my sides and my legs were tight together.'

She described how the vehicle drove off. She felt that two of the men were alongside her, holding her in place as they turned several corners, drove along a straight road for a while then through a number of bends before stopping.

'How long did this go on for?' I asked.

'Not very long really. About ten minutes, but it could have been less. I was so frightened that it was hard to tell.'

When the van stopped, she was pulled out as quickly as she was put in, she told us, hoisted overhead again, carried a short distance and put down on her feet. The bag remained on her head throughout the whole time, but now the cling film was unwrapped and to her horror all of her clothes including her shoes and tights were removed. At last she was naked except for the bag.

'It was very cold, and I was afraid to fight, because all the time one of them was undressing me others were holding me still, and when I was undressed I could feel that all four of them had their hands on me, tight on my arms and round my knees and on my shoulders.'

Betty's stories can be full of imaginative details, but the next part was the weirdest of all. Clare, sitting on Betty's other side, tried to take her hand, but Betty gently pushed her away. I was waiting, my teeth and fists clenched, for what would come next.

'All the time they were doing this,' said Betty, 'I was standing on shingle, and I could hear the sea.'

218

There was silence in the room, except that I could hear a high-pitched whistle inside my head. After a while I heard Clare say, 'But where could you have been Betty? You said it was only ten minutes.'

'It was the sea. I heard the waves break on the shore, then that rattling sucking noise that the shingle makes as it pulls back. Over and over. I know it. And I could feel the shingle under my feet. And it felt colder from the direction of the waves. I'm not sure but I think I could even feel the spray a bit on my body. Then as I stood there, I felt one of them draw something on my back, like a symbol of some sort.'

'Show me,' I said. She leaned forward and pulled up her sweater. Of course her back was clean and unmarked.

After a few moments, she went on. The men had picked her up again, but this time carried her gently in their arms, and walked the few steps back to put her into the van. The journey seemed a little longer this time she said, and because she was no longer wrapped, three of them held her tightly, one with his hands on her lower legs, and two lying close along each side holding her in what she described as a firm embrace. She was, of course, still naked.

All of this time, not one of them had spoken.

'I suddenly knew that it was some kind of ritual,' she said. 'They had not hurt me, and it was as if every movement was practised, as if they were dancers. They were all the same height. I could feel that the ones lying beside me were strong, with hard muscles.'

At the end of this brief journey, she was again carried a short distance. This time she was made to sit down on a cold surface. One man stood behind her, hands on her shoulders, and suddenly she heard three of them running away from her. A moment later the fourth man pressed hard on her shoulders as if fixing her in place, and then she heard him run too. A second later the sound of the van started, and faded into the distance. Shaking, Betty struggled with the bag, which was held around her neck with strong elastic. When she pulled it off, she found she was sitting on our own back doorstep, looking into the darkness of the garden. Her clothes were neatly folded beside her.

As if exhausted, Betty collapsed onto my shoulder. I hauled her into my lap and held her close. Clare went into her kitchen and came back with three glasses and a bottle of red wine.

I shook my head. 'She's asleep,' I said.

After that evening there were two terrible days. I could not in honesty behave as if I believed her. At first Betty cried and sulked, or pummelled me in frustration. I wanted to tell her I believed her, I wanted to say, Let's go to the police. But every time we picked out from the story the details of helmets, cling film, invisible symbol, shingle and the sea, she stopped me.

'I know they won't believe me. If you don't no-one will,' she cried. 'I wish they had hurt me, then there would be more chance.'

Between the bouts of weeping and anger there was a state of collapse, and she slept more and more, sustained only by the sweet tea I gave her at regular intervals. I excused myself from work on the Monday morning, on the basis that I could write the conference report at home. Betty appeared at about ten o'clock, pale and red-eyed.

'I feel so ill,' she said.

'It's no wonder. You've cried yourself into exhaustion. I'll tell them there'll be no rehearsals for a day or two, shall I?'

She nodded weakly. 'Dan, do you think I'm mad?'

I hesitated just too long. Before I could speak, she nodded, an expression of great sadness on her face.

'I don't know, Betty,' I replied. 'I don't think 'mad' is a word that is used nowadays. I think the story-telling, lies I should say, is an obsession, and you've had a problem for a long time.'

Again she nodded. 'On Friday I know I believed what happened, but now it's sort of faded, as if it was a very frightening dream. If it was, it could happen again, couldn't it? I'm really scared. Dan, get help for me, please.'

My feelings were a mixture of feeling desperately sorry for her and relief that now she would go to the therapists that I had found for her. At first, it was agreed that her delusion had been so vivid that she need proper psychiatric treatment, and that was hard. But as the weeks went by and she moved into the care of a wonderful counsellor, who encouraged her to talk about her jealousy of Baby, the lack of boundaries in her indulgent childhood, and the loss of her quiet ineffectual father, a new Betty emerged. She was quieter, reflective, more content. Towards the end of the first year of treatment we were married, and she began to work again.

Her more mature insights had unexpected benefits; she was seen as having a wider range and the roles she was offered reflected that.

Now, nearly ten years later, the terrible time seems to have been a sort of gateway. Our two young sons are being brought up with lots of affection, but clear rules of behaviour including an emphasis on telling the truth. We are happy.

I do wonder occasionally if I should feel guilty about inflicting that experience on her. It cost me a lot of money, of course, but every detail was carried out to the letter. The route of the van was a figure eight through Camden and Chalk Farm, starting and ending on the quiet side street outside our garden door. The shingle (a bag from the local garden centre) was a small patch filling a space at the edge of the patio, and I had made the recording of the sea at Aldeburgh myself. The welders' helmets and the cling film and the ultimate gentleness of the four young Romanians added to the sense of fantasy. I certainly did not want Betty to be hurt, and I was careful about the fairly large doses of trazadone that I put in her tea during those first two days, giving her enough to ensure sleepiness, slight confusion and vivid dreams. It used up all of that year's bonus, but the quarter of a million pounds bought silence from the Romanians and got them safely to the USA, which was what they wanted. Cruel to be kind, or the ends justifying the means, I guess.

A Weighty Problem

It took almost three months of work for Henry and his grandfather George to complete their task. Throughout his professional life George had kept detailed records of the projects he had worked on, but this had, over the years, grown into a mountain of paper. There were dozens of cardboard files, towers of plastic boxes, and drawers full of hard-backed notebooks.

After Grandma Jessica died, Henry persuaded George that he needed to occupy himself, and updating the storage of his work would be a useful and engrossing job. George agreed. By this time, 2035, paper had become obsolete; in his own study, surrounded by all this evidence of a life spent in the pursuit of science, he could smell the mustiness, the onset of decay. Henry's computer was a better destination, and George was impressed to find that a thousand pages of his research could be transferred to a disk the size of a five pound coin.

Of course, a great deal of time had to be spent in deciding what should be saved, and in what form. Henry pointed out that every page could be scanned in seconds but that it would be a mind-numbingly boring job doing nothing but feed endless sheets into the machine. Henry's method was to spread the contents of each box out over the largest floor area in the house, take a digital photo, transfer this to the computer, where with conversion software it could be digitally labeled then disked. This way a box could be completed in a day.

Sometimes, George would become engrossed in reminiscing over some particularly significant experiment. He would try to engage Henry in this, but the boy had his own agenda. As the material passed through the computer, he was performing rapid searches for a few specific words and phrases. He knew which aspects of his grandfather's work might be important in the future.

If the purpose of the task had been to rouse George from the trough of sadness into which he had fallen after Jessica's death, it worked to a certain extent. He remembered, and re-lived, the emotions he had experienced at certain times, the pride and happiness of great success, the relief when near failure was turned to advantage, or at least disaster had been averted. George's work had been almost exclusively in pharmaceutical research, and he had been involved in some of the great advances of the late 20th and early 21st century.

There had been frustrations too. Early in his career, in the mid 1980s, as a bright young chemist straight from Cambridge, he had worked on the development of a particular hydrochloride mono hydrate salt, being developed as an anti-depressant. The work had been stopped during clinical trials. George was disappointed, though he recognised the need for extreme caution. Unwilling to let all of his careful work be lost, he had recorded the formulation, results and side effects. This was the beginning of something which he acknowledged as something of an obsession.

This early time in George's working life was familiar to Henry. The story had been told to him, in the manner of a cautionary tale, when he was much younger. One may work hard, then be disappointed, but one must not allow that disappointment to be discouraging. Henry had

227

remembered the lesson, and now had an urgent reason to find the working records, and as many others as could be discovered amongst his grandfather's papers. As they transferred onto his computer, Henry activated a number of search terms, including 'weight loss', 'obesity', 'Type 2 diabetes'. One after another the experiments appeared; anti-depressant (side effect weight loss), sedative (side effect weight loss), laxative (side effect weight loss), hypertension (side effect weight loss). Henry was interested in the ones that had been stopped at clinical trial or shortly after going into production, and therefore forgotten. He felt sure that there would be a common factor, or combination, that would serve his purpose.

Henry was a victim of the obesity generation. Both his parents had died of diabetes-related conditions in their thirties, when he was almost too young to remember them. George's son Callum had a sudden fatal heart attack, and Miriam his wife contracted an antibiotic-resistant infection through a gangrenous foot. Neither of them had taken seriously the advice that their life of inactivity, takeaway food, snacks, smoking and compulsive television-watching would almost certainly kill them. Although this seemed something of a tragedy at the time, their fate was far from unusual. By 2020 even cautious statistics showed that more than eighty per cent of adults under the age of forty were overweight or obese, and of those, half were diagnosed as diabetic or pre-diabetic. Callum and Miriam also belonged to an identifiable group for whom the risk was exaggerated – they had stressful jobs which were done at home. Twelve hours a day sitting at a screen, followed by an exhausted evening, contributed to their downfall. As a nod in the direction of taking his fitness more seriously Callum had a phone app that counted his steps; on too many days the number barely reached three figures. After a while he came to believe that one thousand steps a day would keep him agile. Miriam regularly paid for an online exercise class, and once in a while puffed through the warm-up. Their lifestyle was effectively slow suicide.

Sadly, children of Henry's generation were not protected from this. The big body had become normal, and the gloomy warning that these children would have shorter lives than their parents, and considerably shorter than their grandparents, became a sort of background noise in society. When Henry began his own research, out of the kind of macabre interest in death that afflicts many teenagers, he had read about an interesting social phenomenon. About the time of George's young adulthood there had been an epidemic, not of fatness, but of extreme thinness. In dealing with anorexia in teenaged girls, a belief had sprung up that it was dangerous to draw attention to overweight in youngsters. Referring to a child as chubby, or any other euphemism, was deemed to be an invitation to embark on a regime of self-starvation. 'Fat' was the ultimate insult, a word that provoked shock. Henry thought, 'I bet lard was a really bad swear word then,' and smiled to himself. It was one of his favourite words. So the obesity spread. And after all, it could not be denied that in any hospital the majority of the staff were hugely overweight. If numbers represented normality, then it became normal to be large, lethargic, and depressed enough to lack motivation for change.

Fortunately for Henry his grandparents, who took over responsibility for him, had a more enlightened attitude, being of the generation born in the 1960s, so his upbringing was somewhat old-fashioned. Only in one aspect did Henry follow the example of his parents, but to excess; by the age of sixteen he was brilliantly knowledgeable and skilful in everything that could be done with his computer.

So, the weeks passed and the work was done. All the information was transferred, George had dictated his hand-written notes and the computer had stored them as documents, then as tiny disks. Henry had extracted all the information he required, and had a new task for his grandfather.

'All of these pieces of information that I've extracted, Granddad, are about compounds you developed that reduce weight. I know that in every case another outcome was being pursued, but why was this useful stuff thrown out as well as the rest?'

'It wasn't always,' George replied. 'See this experiment here. The antidepressant that was being worked on caused some nerve damage, but this part of the formula, ' he pointed to a molecular diagram, 'was a perfectly functional fat binder, and was available as such for quite a few years. But the trouble with that, and nearly all of the other things you've picked out, is that they aren't magic potions. All the instructions that went with the ones that did get used contained the depressing words "Works in conjunction with a calorie controlled diet".

That means will-power and self-denial and nobody wants anything to do with that.' He added bitterly, 'I don't exclude your father from that, and over the years I've asked myself how I was to blame for allowing my son to go down that path. It looked as if everyone of his generation, and since, has wanted nothing that doesn't come easily. D'you know, when your Dad was a teenager, some government department did a survey asking hundreds of twelve to sixteen-year-olds what their ambition was for adulthood. A few said they wanted to be teachers, or doctors or plumbers or musicians or whatever, but the most common answers were "famous" or "rich". No plan for how to get there, no mention of study or hard work. Magic potions, that's what they wanted.'

Henry turned back to the screen. 'I suppose these weight reducing drugs worked in a variety of ways, Granddad. Do you suppose that if combinations of them were made, they would be effective enough to make weight loss easier?'

'Oh yes, that would be, well, not simple, because working out just how the molecules would react would take a bit of work. But I've always known that it would be possible. This here, and this one that works on the part of the brain that controls appetite, together with this oxide that affects taste, could be combined to have that result. Add a bit of laxative, and the results would start to be obvious in a couple of weeks.'

'Why has it never been done?'

'I suppose I'm the only person who has kept all of these results. Ten of the twenty or so that you've picked out come from programs that were immensely costly, so when the primary purpose failed the companies just couldn't afford to do anything but ditch them. Like I said, one or two got developed and used for a while. This one, sibutramine, had a short life as a weight loss drug, but most of them just disappeared. Also, not many people worked on so many of the programs that I was involved with. I guess this collection has never been put together by anyone else.'

'Could you do it, Granddad? Now that we have all the information, could you calculate how to use this information?'

'I could,' George said slowly. 'I can think of a few combinations that I could devise.'

'Without laboratory facilities?'

'Of course. The experiments have been done. It's effectively a mathematical task now. But the dangers are still there, you know. If there was a ten per cent chance of cardiovascular problems then, there still would be now. The combinations that would work best would have to stimulate the metabolism, which isn't always a good plan in someone with potential heart problems.'

Henry grimaced impatiently. 'Some of those dangers came from the components that weren't to do with weight loss though. And being a great fat lard-arse with diabetes, heart failure, no legs, going blind, kidney failure; all that's quite dangerous too.'

George nodded. 'True. Well, it would be a good intellectual exercise. But why have you got so interested in this?'

Henry grinned. 'We're going to save the world. I've even thought of a name. NoBesity.'

His grandfather laughed. 'You're a funny boy Henry. But it's better than some hobbies, I guess.'

Henry shook his head. 'This is a bit more than a hobby, Granddad. If I tell you something I've done, will you promise to keep it a secret?'

'Depends. What is it?'

Henry sighed. 'I've got a television program I would like you to watch. It's one of that Question series you like, but you won't have seen it. Er... not many people have. You see I er... well, I hacked into the NewBBC and I found this particular one that had turned out a bit too controversial to be aired.'

'You did what...?'

'Yes, I know, but if you'll just watch it, or a bit of it, you'll see why I need your help.'

Henry turned back to the computer, tapped the touch screen rapidly, then made room for George to sit beside him. The familiar mix of politicians, scientists and broadcasters appeared on the screen, sitting on an almost circular sofa, the presenter Jonas Jonasson in the middle. Three of the participants were regulars, Clara Smithers the well-known broadcaster and medical journalist, Pierre Lunaire, epidemiologist, and Grant Fortune, former shadow Home Secretary. The visiting panellists were Esther Mixx, Secretary of State for Ethical Technology, Bridget Fallow, Hawking Professor of Cosmology, and Peter Goodwin, poet and gerontologist.

'Good team,' remarked George. 'That Mixx woman was excellent when the NHS chip recognition system went

235

down and a million people had to go back to injecting insulin for several days.' He settled back in his chair and prepared to watch. 'But you say this episode wasn't shown. Do you know why?'

Henry tapped again and the image jumped rapidly forwards. 'You'll understand soon. It was a security thing. I think this is where the tricky bit began.'

Jonasson was speaking. 'Esther, you put some of the blame historically on Mrs. May's snap election way back in '17.'

'Yes. It was the outcome of that election and the events that followed that gave rise to the emergence of the More Conservative Party. That notorious phenomenon, the unexpected consequence. An undertaking to reduce the so-called 'immigrant' population. The racist majority spoke, the government declared a democratic imperative to do as The People demanded, and as a result almost a third of NHS hospital doctors were sent back to their countries of origin. I suppose The People had in mind the faceless women wearing the burka, the gangs of black teenagers, oh we all know the targets. But in order to reach the required numbers a whole swathe of essential professions was lost. The People weren't so pleased then, but the damage was done. '

Grant Fortune stirred uncomfortably. 'Esther is right. Subsequent governments, including at the time when I was in opposition, tried desperately to reverse the trend, but of course countries like India welcomed their returning emigrants with open arms, gave them the respect they never really had here. The resulting improvement in health programs there, and, for example, in the Philippines where hundreds of highly trained nurses turned up, completely changed those countries. With some of the best health care and associated education, they have become major players on the world stage, while we struggle on with these massive … and I use the word deliberately… difficulties.'

Jonasson smiled. 'We take your point Grant. But that's history. We're looking at the current state of our economy, and how improvements in the Health Service can solve some of this government's problems. Clara, you and your fellow journalists have a wider view of the situation. Leaving the history aside, how do you see society's woes nowadays?'

'I don't believe you can ignore the history,' Dr. Smithers replied. 'I remember my grandfather, who was a statistician working for one of the big insurance companies, telling me that as early as the 1960s he was involved in discussions about imbalance in society. He could see that it would not be long before there was a situation in which the number of old people greatly outnumbered the number of young. Of course, the insurance companies were looking at it from the point of view of providing pensions...'

'Oh God, pensions,' chipped in Grant. 'How can you get people to understand how that works? The number of times I've had to take on someone who says 'I paid in all my working life, so now I'm entitled'. You cannot get them to understand that their contribution was paying the pensions of the generation older, and that their own pension depended on the young people working now. I practically had to draw diagrams of 1948 to show that people who were old then and became entitled to the new state pension were paid out of current taxation, and that's how it's always been.'

Peter Goodwin sat forward. 'It was always thought that extending life, or at least having a healthy old age for as long as possible was a basic aim for the Health Service, but while we were achieving that, this horrible epidemic of ill health was overtaking the young.'

'Epidemic is now an understatement,' chipped in Lunaire.

'Self-inflicted,' muttered Goodwin.

'You can say that,' replied Lunaire, 'but it is the situation, and solutions need to be found.'

'Maybe like Japan?' This was Mixx.

Jonasson asked, 'What about Japan? Nobody knows much about Japan nowadays.'

'Another of the unexpected consequences,' said Fortune. 'After racist opinion was allowed to run rife, countries became inward-looking, borders closed. Japan became more or less impenetrable to the rest of the world. I think the Japanese solution has been suspected for a while, and since those smuggled Instadisk recordings many of us know.'

'Know what?' Jonasson looked puzzled.

'The cull. Japan was the first country to publicise the fact that its old population had outnumbered the young. About 2015 or 16 I think it was. Once their government found that it could keep out the eyes of the world, they started rectifying that.'

'Of course,' said Dr. Smithers. 'The Japanese are the politest, kindliest race until that ceases to work. Then the underlying ruthlessness emerges. Look again at history and World War 2. I believe the cut-off age was 75.'

Jonasson looked up, horrified. 'You mean... the old people were just... killed!'

'Don't be naïve, Jonas. To some extent it's happening all over the world. There's been some kind of tacit undercover agreement to look the other way.' Smithers smiled and shrugged. 'It's a long time since we started the process here in the UK. The first step was early this century, a strong message that our society could not afford old people.'

'What message?' Bridget Fallow spoke for the first time. 'I'm older than all of you and I don't remember anything like that.'

'Oh it wasn't an overt threat,' replied Smithers. 'There was a reclassification of what it meant to be old. Suddenly the age at which one became a pensioner changed; no longer 60 for women and 65 for men. What is that but a statement that society can't afford you to be old? Government needed you to work, earn and pay taxes for far longer. Your age for becoming old extended and extended, until there was a tipping point at which older people were costing the state more in support and health care than they would have done as normal pensioners. So the obvious solution is to get rid of them.'

At this point Jonasson stood up and turned to the camera. 'Cut this,' he said. 'This can't go on. We'll take a break and start on the next subject. Online schools.'

Henry touched the screen and the picture disappeared. When he turned to look at his grandfather he saw that George was pale and shocked.

'Sorry Granddad, I know it's hard to take in, but I'm sure it's true. I started to wonder about it two years ago when I was only fourteen. Remember I did my Prince George Scheme volunteering in the care home. The old people were really nice, but I was puzzled why there weren't any really old ones, only a couple over seventy five, and they disappeared, died somewhere else during my first week. That happened regularly, even to people who weren't at all obviously ill. It was always reported as something sudden, like a heart attack or a stroke. Then one day I got the chance to use their computer. The manager asked me to do an online grocery order. But it was dead easy for me to have a look at some files that were partly encrypted, and I saw that every time one of the old folk died there was a 'compensation' payment from the government, exactly equivalent to one year's fee for residents. I was thinking about it ever since, then I found that TV programme.'

'So everyone over seventy five…?'

'I think it's a bit younger than that now, I'm afraid.' Henry sighed and grimaced. 'I hoped I would avoid telling you this, but I think Grandma Jessica…'.

'No, no, don't say she was murdered.'

'You can't say that. It's only murder if it's against the law, and this isn't. It's a government policy.'

'How do you know?'

'I hacked into her chip, about a month before she died.'

'What chip?'

'I suppose I was already suspicious, and then I just couldn't see the logic about the flu vaccinations. All of a sudden they were compulsory last winter, when no-one had bothered much before. So I'm thinking, they are killing people at one end and at the other telling everyone over sixty that if they don't have this vaccine that will save their lives they'll go to jail. So I scanned her and I found it. Quite a simple little device with an alert on it with her birth date.'

'But she was a year younger than me. How come I'm still here?'

'I guess they can't just bump everyone off the moment they hit a certain age, which I think is now sixty five by the way. There's probably a randomised selection process.'

'So I could go at any time?'

'In theory, but Granddad, I've hacked yours as well, and mmm ... I've adjusted your age. As far as the government's computers are concerned you are sixty, and I can keep you there indefinitely. I can't make you any younger because if you were, you wouldn't have the chip.'

'So why are we wasting all this time on my research papers?'

'Well, my thinking is, I'm not actually clever enough to alter the killing program, but if we can produce something that makes all the fat younger people healthy and productive again, the imbalance will be corrected, and the older people will be saved. Better get busy.'

George was stunned. 'But it will take years for a new piece of research to have that kind of effect. What's the point?'

'Better late than never, don't you think? And anyway, it needn't take years. I've located a policy that the government is supporting, paying for in other words, that has a whole range of projects ready to put into practice, some legislation about food, some education, some about grants to hospitals that run anti-obesity programs and do gastro-intestinal surgery. When you come up with the formula, I can insert it as part of that program and it will be put into practice within months. You'll just not have to mind not getting the credit.'

'Well…' Like most research scientists George had a deeply ingrained desire for his work to be recognised and rewarded.

"Don't forget you'll be saving your own life, as well as all the lardboxes that will get healthy.'

George needed space to think. Henry decided to go out for a while, which was something he didn't much enjoy. Although they lived in what had been a respectable and quiet part of Cambridge, the streets were never entirely free of groups of annoying kids. They were rarely actually dangerous, just bored and slightly angry. Nearly all state education was delivered online, and in homes where there was no adult with sufficient energy to enforce participation, the programs were ignored. Henry had heard many times George's explanation for this state of affairs. 'Who wanted to be a teacher in the 20s, for goodness sake? No disciplining allowed, kids running roughshod, classes of fifty. Schools just died out and no wonder'. So Henry had been unusual in completing his online education, supplemented by input from his grandparents, and the use of a state of the art computer.

There was a street of old-fashioned shops nearby, run by Social History for England, a tourist destination since all shopping had been done online since about 2025. Each had the appearance of a shop of the 1950s with real produce, a counter, and people behind it to take fingerprint payment. Security was tight, in the form of wireless surveillance and a patrolling guard. Henry wandered along to the cake shop to get a reward for George if the work had started by the time he got back. Trillionaire's shortbread was their favourite. He kept an eye open for the gangs of kids, though he was no more than mildly nervous. After all, he was thin and healthy and could run.

When Henry returned George was bent over one of his old notebooks, a page already half covered with calculations and diagrams. He grinned at Henry. 'I'll enjoy this,' he said, 'I've got two or three possibilities in mind that could work. And when it is saving the world, as you say, someone might want to know who was behind it. I could go down in history in the end.'

It took only just over a week for George to produce two complete formulations for drugs that would bring about rapid loss of weight, at the rate of between five and ten kilos a week, more or less depending on the starting weight.

'Formula A,' he told Henry, 'works more quickly, but causes some digestive problems. There's an ingredient that used to be active in a product called Fleet, which basically turns everything in your gut to yellow water. It used to be used to clear the bowel before colonoscopy, and the patient would be told not to leave the house because it causes urgent need for the lavatory. So it's tricky, but helps to keep whatever is ingested moving at such a speed that little of it is assimilated. I'd advise use on alternate days as it does rather interfere with nutrition. There are other ingredients to do with metabolism, but I've been cautious because the combination could be a bit of a disaster for anyone with certain heart conditions.

'Formula B,' he went on, 'is even more effective, perhaps up to twelve kilos a week in a really obese person, but risky in a different way. It has a dual action, one of which alters signals in the part of the brain that controls appetite, and that can potentially cause some nerve damage in unpredictable parts of the body. About 10% chance of that. It also prevents the absorption of sugar from whatever source, while at the same time allowing the secretion of leptin, which suppresses appetite. This element here prevents the action of lactase, so that sugars cannot enter the bloodstream. Clever, yes?'

'You've lost me Granddad. So either would work, but A is more likely to kill people than B?'

'Both a bit dicey, to be honest, because with a morbidly obese person the drug would have to be taken for a long time, and there would be a whole lot of health risks through loss of nutrients. But with medical oversight, either would be worth a try.'

Henry was quietly excited. There was just one more secret aspect to his plan. After he had transferred George's formulae to disk, he poured a modest Scotch for George and a Diet Punchball for himself. 'Here's to you Granddad, Scientist of the Year. Tomorrow I'll upload all of this into the government Health Program, and we can then wait to observe the results.'

George was tired after his mental exertions. After he had gone to bed and was sound asleep, Henry made several more copies of the formulae, ensuring that each was encrypted differently, but that every one was prefaced with a reference to his grandfather's will, in which all of George's property, both material and intellectual was left to Henry his grandson. Then he went to the program which had enabled him to read George's implant. Here he adjusted the information to ensure that at 2.37 a.m. the Government cull program would take effect and George would suffer a sudden and catastrophic electrical storm in his brain, with the same symptoms and result as a fatal stroke.

Job done, thought Henry.

*

Acknowledgements

There are times when I realize how little I understand about what goes on in my computer, so I am very grateful to my clever friend, Doc David Turner.

Nothing is more encouraging than a friend who says a story made her laugh out loud, so thank you Clair.

And a longsuffering husband is an asset too. That's Keith.

Printed in Great Britain
by Amazon